Runaway Cowboy

Also by T. J. Kline

Learning the Ropes
The Cowboy and the Angel
Rodeo Queen

Runaway Cowboy

T. J. KLINE

This is a work of fiction. Names, characters, places, and incidents are products of the author's imagination or are used fictitiously and are not to be construed as real. Any resemblance to actual events, locales, organizations, or persons, living or dead, is entirely coincidental.

Excerpt from *Learning the Ropes* copyright © 2014 by Tina Klinesmith.

Excerpt from *Various States of Undress: Georgia* copyright © 2014 by Laura Simcox.

Excerpt from *Make It Last* copyright © 2014 by Megan Erickson.

Excerpt from *Hero By Night* copyright © 2014 by Sara Jane Stone.

Excerpt from *Mayhem* copyright © 2014 by Jamie Shaw.

Excerpt from *Sinful Rewards 1* copyright © 2014 by Cynthia Sax.

Excerpt from *Forbidden* copyright © 2014 by Charlotte Stein.

Excerpt from *Her Highland Fling* copyright © 2014 by Jennifer McQuiston.

EPub Edition FEBRUARY 2015 ISBN: 9780062370112

Print Edition ISBN: 9780062370129

AM 10 9 8 7 6 5 4 3 2 1

*For Michelle who reminds me every day
to push myself beyond my limits and
how important it is to laugh.
And for Aunt Ba who insisted the
next three books be dedicated to her.
I love you both!*

Chapter One

JENNIFER CHANDLER BOLTED upright in the bed of her trailer, waking from her nightmare with a gasp. A fine sheen of sweat covered her body, even in the cool early morning air. She scrubbed her eyes with her hands, brushing her light brown hair back from her face, but she couldn't seem to shake the vision of her mother from her mind. It had been over twelve years since her parents had been killed in an accident, but foggy nights on the road always seemed to give her nightmares. She hated that she could picture her mother's face clearly in these dreams, pleading with Jennifer to save them before the semitruck crossed into their lane, but she couldn't picture her face at any other time, no matter how hard she tried.

Jen flipped back the covers and dropped her legs over the side of the mattress, wondering if she should just get up now. Sleep would probably elude her for the rest of the night anyway. She'd take a sleepless night over falling back into that nightmare again any time. Her feet padded on the carpet as she made her way to the small kitchenette to start coffee. She glanced at the clock over the stove. It wasn't even five in the morning, but she might as well head out to feed the animals a little early and save her brothers the work.

She reached for her youngest brother's sweatshirt, which hung on the back of the chair, and went to check on him. Derek was sleeping soundly on the sofa bed, his hands curled under the pillow. She brushed his dark hair back from his face, as her heart swelled with love for him. She knew it drove him nuts when she mothered him, but she couldn't help it. When their parents died, she'd tried to band her siblings together as tightly as possible, and because she was the oldest, she'd taken on a parenting role for both of her younger brothers. Just because Derek was in college now didn't mean she wouldn't still watch out for him.

Jennifer reached for the flashlight and slipped out the door as quietly as possible, cringing when it creaked loudly. She added asking Jake, the rodeo crew foreman, to oil the hinges to her mental to-do list. She shivered as the chill from the low fog crept into the folds of her sweatshirt, and she tugged it around her tighter. She might hate being on the road in this kind of weather, but as a stock contractor, the rodeo season was the way they made their living, rain or shine…or fog. She set the flashlight on top of the alfalfa and reached for the clippers to cut the twine. The feeling of dread from her nightmare was clinging to her like a cobweb. Logically, she knew the chance of the same sort of accident happening to them again was one in a million, but even those odds were too great for her. Honestly, the traveling was the only part of the job she *didn't* like. She broke off several flakes of hay.

"I thought I heard someone out here."

She spun, knocking the flashlight to the ground and biting back a curse at her jumpiness. "Scott," she whispered, trying to keep from waking the others still sleeping nearby. "You scared me."

"Sorry," he said, stepping forward to pick up the flashlight from where it still spun, illuminating their feet in turn through the haze. "You all right?"

"Yeah," she muttered as she took the flashlight from her brother. "Did I wake you?"

He cocked his head to the side. "Jen, I'm a grown man. Just because Derek lets you baby him doesn't mean I will."

Lately, her brothers couldn't seem to be in the same room and get along. Sure, Derek was immature and tended to skip out on the work whenever possible, but Scott had become bitter and angry at the world after breaking off his engagement. Jen gave Scott an understanding smile as she arched her brow. "I'm not trying to mother you. But you have to be on horseback all day. I don't. Go back to bed."

"It's fine, I'm already up." Scott reached for two flakes of alfalfa and carried them to the cattle pen. "Another nightmare?"

She turned to look at him, surprised. "How did you know?"

"I've known for years." He didn't elaborate, but she could hear the sympathy in his voice. "Jen, you've got to stop living in the past. I miss Mom and Dad, too, but they're gone."

"I'm not living in the past, Scott. I'm trying to plan for the future, and that includes making sure we are all taken care of, no matter what might happen." She reached for the hay.

"You're awfully pessimistic this morning. I thought that was my job around here."

She rolled her eyes at him. Still, she glanced around as the fog settled close to the ground, making the cattle look like eerie ghosts, shifting in the haze of the early predawn light. She shivered slightly, but this time, it wasn't from the cold. "I sure hope this burns off."

"It's California. It'll probably end up in the eighties." Scott took the flakes of alfalfa from her hands. "Go start the coffee. I'll take care of the animals. We both know I can't cook, and if I try, I'll just make a mess in your trailer. Then the crew will go hungry and be meaner than those bulls."

Jen grinned. "Already done, baby brother, but I'll go get you some."

"Stop calling me that," he grumbled.

She took the chance, while his hands were full and he couldn't retaliate, to pinch his cheek playfully. "Aw, you'll always be my baby brother." She laughed as he glared at her and hurried back to her trailer.

Jen opened the door to see Derek had flopped onto his back, one arm flung across his eyes, snoring loudly.

She was just pouring coffee for herself and Scott when she heard a quiet knock on the door. Mike opened it and came inside, stealing Scott's cup.

"Morning, Mike." She leaned over and kissed the old man's cheek before fetching another mug for Scott.

All three of the siblings adored Mike. He'd given up his own plans for the future to accept guardianship when their parents were killed. Mike had been more than a partner to their father; he'd been his best friend, rodeo partner, and—after their father's death—the man helping her brothers navigate the path to manhood.

"Morning, kiddo. You doing okay?"

Jen could read the worry in his watery blue eyes. He saw too much and knew her too well. "Rough night," she admitted.

"I know this weekend's gonna be hard for you, but I'm here if you need to talk."

Jen frowned, wondering about his cryptic offer, until she remembered the date: March 25, the anniversary of her parents' death. The heaviness that had hung over her since waking began to seep into her bones.

"Could you two talk quieter? Some of us are trying to sleep," Derek groaned from the bed, breaking through the painful memories threatening to bury her.

"Sorry, Derek, but that's what you get for crashing in the big, comfy trailer instead of the smaller ones like the rest of us guys."

"Gee, thanks for the sympathy, Mike." He swung his long legs over the side of the bed and ran his hands through his messy hair. "I do you a favor, come home from school this weekend to help out, and this is the thanks I get?"

"Get up and help out then, ya spoiled brat," Mike teased. Derek chuckled at the ribbing. "I'm sure your brother could use some help feeding," Mike added more seriously.

"Fine." Derek sighed as he pulled a wrinkled T-shirt over his lanky frame and stuffed his feet into the worn cowboy boots he'd tucked under the bed. "I'm going. Maybe I should've just stayed at school this weekend," he muttered as he walked to the door.

"Here, take this." Jen handed him the sweatshirt. "It's freezing out there."

He slid his arms into the warmth as she shivered; the air in the trailer was colder than she'd expected. "Thanks, Jen. I'll be back for coffee, too."

The pair watched him leave. "You think he's ever going to grow up, Mike?"

"Give him some room and a reason, kiddo. Derek's going to turn out just fine. So will Scott." He turned to face her, and she wondered how he always seemed to know exactly what she was thinking. "That daughter of mine did a real number on that boy, and I'm ashamed to say I'm to blame for the way things turned out."

Jen reached over and squeezed his hand. "Liz made her own choices. You did the best you could. Look how good you've done with us. Here." She handed him a cup of steaming coffee. "Take this out to Scott?"

CLAYTON GRAHAM LOOKED around the rodeo arena. He knew Jennifer was around here somewhere; he just wasn't sure if he was trying to find her or avoid her. It'd been almost five years since he'd last seen her, sleeping peacefully next to him with her hand tucked under her chin, wearing the engagement ring he'd slipped on her finger only hours before. Then he had walked out the bedroom door and out of her life.

A tall cowboy on a black and white paint jogged his horse past him, barely glancing his way before he pulled the horse up short. The animal's hind feet slid in the packed dirt.

"Clay?" The rider spun the horse and headed back toward him. "Holy crap, it *is* you!"

"Scott?" Clay looked up at the man on the horse. "You've filled out."

Scott dismounted and threw his arm out for a handshake. "Forget that, man, get over here." Clay wrapped a massive arm around the younger man's shoulder in a quick one-armed hug. At one time, Scott had been his best friend, his confidante, and almost his brother-in-law.

"Well, five years added some meat to my scrawny bones." Scott chuckled. "What have you been up to?"

He shrugged. "Riding, roping. I'm working as a pickup man for Smith Brothers up in Oregon now."

Clay appreciated that Scott didn't seem to be holding any grudges about the way he had snuck out and run away, but he'd called later to explain as much as he could to Scott and Mike, swearing them to silence. He didn't think Jen was going to be so gracious about having been abandoned without a word. He shook off his doubts. He'd been right to end it the way he had—a clean break—to let her move on with her life and forget him. Even if he couldn't forget her.

"That explains why you're built like a Mack truck now," Scott said, slapping at Clay's arm. "So, what are you doing here?"

"Hazing for a couple friends who came down from Oregon to ride." He glanced around. "Is Mike around?"

"Somewhere, probably up in the announcer's booth getting ready." Scott shot him a wary glance. "You haven't talked to Jen yet, have you?"

Clay wondered if Scott was warning him off or trying to discern his intentions. "I just got here. Do I need to keep my distance?"

Scott shrugged a shoulder and hopped back into the saddle. "I would if I were you. Unless you're planning on explaining why you disappeared." He shook his head as his horse pranced in place. "Then again, you weren't always the brightest cowboy on the ranch. Listen, I've got to run, but hang around after. We'll catch up."

Scott was gone before Clay could tell him he'd rather get this ride over and get out before Jen found out he was even there.

What he needed to do was find out where Dustin, Cody, and Chase—the friends he was hazing for—were. He'd taken time off and dragged his butt and his horses down here for them, so the least they could do was show up on time. He pulled his cell phone from his back pocket and punched in Cody's number, growing more irate with each ring. When Cody's voice mail picked up, Clay sighed into the phone and didn't bother leaving a message.

Chances were that all three of them were either hungover or with some groupies they met at a truck stop along the way. Leave it to those three to find a way to make a two-hour road trip into a weekend bender. He never should have taken the chance on driving down here and coming face to face with the one woman he'd never forgotten. He knew better than anyone that running was the only way to stay one step ahead of the trouble that seemed to follow his family.

He shoved his phone back into his pocket and adjusted his hat, looking around at the sea of horse trailers. He might as well get the horses saddled, since it looked like those three would be dragging their asses in right before the bulldogging event. He turned back toward his trailer but stopped short when he saw her. She was riding her red roan, Jiggy, the one he had helped her break and train. Her light brown hair hung in long waves down her back, kissed by the sunlight, and glistening like burnished gold beneath her black cowboy hat. She was lining up sponsor flags at the back gate of the arena, getting ready for the opening ceremonies, and he couldn't help but think about how many hours they'd spent together doing the exact same thing.

The ink on his college degree wasn't even dry when he had begged Mike for a chance to work with him. The business degree was fine, but he wasn't made for an office job. So he'd started as part of the behind-the-scenes chute crew with Findley Brothers, helping with horn wraps, hauling the gates open and closed, and loading the animals. But none of it stopped him from watching

Jen's every move. She was beautiful, even with her hair wound in a long braid down her back, dirt smudging her cheeks, and a large bruise on her forehead from working with a colt who threw her. Her deep chocolate eyes were gentle, and he got lost in them the first time he saw her. The first time he kissed her, he thought he'd found heaven. Then he went and threw it all away.

Clay's eyes traveled the length of her. She'd filled out, developed a woman's curves, and they suited her. As his gaze lit on her face, their eyes met through the throng of cowboys and horses, and he knew she recognized him. Those gentle eyes turned as hard as stone.

No way was she going to be as gracious as Scott had been. She was pissed. This was one cowgirl he was going to have to go out of his way to avoid, because he had a feeling she might be looking for him when his event was over. And it wasn't to rekindle the romance that burned too brightly the first time. She had murder on her mind.

AFTER ALL THESE years, what would possess Clay Graham to show up at one of their rodeos? It had been nearly five years since she saw him last, right after he asked her to marry him. Only a few hours later, he'd turned tail and run, leaving her with a diamond engagement ring and a shattered heart full of memories. No note, no explanation, no returned phone calls. Vanished like this morning's fog in the heat. Oh, he called Mike and Scott to apologize to them. Apparently, both of them meant more to him than she did because she'd never heard from him again.

Her eyes bore into him, wishing looks really could kill. Derek bumped her leg with another sponsor flag from the trailer.

"Um, hello, Jen? You planning on taking this or do I need to walk it over myself?"

"Clay's here."

"Your Clay? Where? I haven't seen him in forever." He sounded excited instead of enraged. Was a little loyalty from her brothers too much to expect?

"Wow, Derek, thanks for the support. That ass abandoned me—all of us—in the middle of the night." She jerked the flag from her brother's hands. "By all means, go see him, have fun. Maybe the two of you can swap rodeo stories, hang out, talk about old times."

Derek shoved his hands into his pockets, looking contrite. "Aw, come on, Jen. Don't be mad at me." He looked up at her, pouting slightly. "I didn't mean it that way. I'd barely started learning to drive when he left. I was just a kid. Want me to go kick his ass?" he offered, grinning.

She could never stay mad at Derek, especially when he teased her. He might not pull his weight around the rodeos, or at the ranch for that matter, but he was charming, and he knew exactly how to worm his way into her good graces. "No. I think I can manage to ignore him." She glanced back to where her ex stood, watching her. "Besides, if anyone gets to kick his sorry ass, it's *me*."

"Well, just let me know if you need backup." He winked at his sister. "But, right now, you'd better hurry up and get these flags where they belong, or Scott will have both our heads. I'm already in enough trouble with him."

She cocked her head and looked down at him from atop the horse, sighing. "What now? I'm getting tired of playing referee between you two."

"I told him I want to change majors."

"Again? Derek, you've got to stick with something and see it all the way through," she scolded. "You're almost finished now. Why would you want to start over?"

"Because I don't know what I want to do. But I do know what I don't want." He looked around at the bustle of cowboys heading up the stairs toward the chutes, preparing for the first bronc riding event. "This isn't the life I want. The ranch, sure, but I'm tired of trying to live up to Scott's expectations, being the guy everyone wants to take the reins. Running the business has never been my thing. I'm thinking about architecture."

Jennifer sighed again, feeling like she was constantly nagging at him. But Derek had a tendency to look for the easiest path and ignore the fact that anything worthwhile took hard work, dedication, and a little sacrifice.

"This isn't exactly the way I pictured life turning out either. But, sometimes, we have to make the best of what we have." She thought about her nightmare and how much she hated hauling the rigs from rodeo to rodeo, fearful with each turn that someone might cross over the divider and change her life again. "*Rodeo* is what we do, what Mom and Dad did and raised us to do, and Mike needs us. He was there when we needed him. If you want to study something else, go ahead, but at least get your business degree first."

Jen nudged her horse into a jog to the arena gate, casting another glance at the man seated at the opposite end, still watching her. She felt her chest constrict in a knot. Nope, life wasn't fairy tales and happy endings. Most of the time, it was hard work and making the best of situations you'd rather avoid.

Chapter Two

THE SUN BEATING down on his shoulders as he waited for his go-round wasn't nearly as hot as his temper right now. How dare those three bail on him? He'd quit riding the circuit years ago because he was tired of depending on irresponsible "friends" for his paycheck. If he wanted to rodeo, he'd go back to bulldogging and collect the entire purse for himself. Instead he was hazing, using his horses to keep steers in line for guys who didn't even bother to call and let him know they weren't coming after all. Luckily, it wasn't a completely wasted trip. A few guys who knew him begged Clay to haze for them. He patted the shoulder of his mount. Maybe he could at least earn his gas money back from his cut of their winnings.

His eyes slid to the other end of the arena where Jen sat on Scott's paint gelding, Noble, another horse he'd helped them break and train. Sunlight glinted off the golden highlights in her hair, and her profile made her look regal. She lifted her chin up as the announcer called out the rodeo sponsor, and she loped Noble around the arena, the flag snapping in the wind that the animal's speed created. Watching her move with the horse, her hips rocking in time with his gallop, made him think about the last time those thighs were wrapped around him. He felt his irritation cool as his desire heated.

He couldn't help but grin as she rounded the curve of the arena where he waited at the gate. He wondered if she realized he was there. Clay watched her spur the horse, gently asking for more speed as she rounded the turn. Dirt clods kicked up from Noble's hooves, spraying Clay with mud as he ducked his head. He looked up in time to see her glance back at him with a wide smile gracing her full lips, her eyes bright with gratification.

Yep, she noticed you here. Sucker.

Jen had never been able to hide anything, at least not from him, and now was no exception. He could easily read the satisfaction she felt at spraying him with mud, but he could also see the hurt she was trying to hide. She wore her heart in those dark eyes. Eyes so dark and fathomless, a guy could lose himself for days. Which was part of why he'd had to leave. Before he lost himself to her completely.

"Clay, you coming?" the steer wrestler asked as he went through the gate.

Clay stared at Jen, tipping two fingers against his hat, and watched the laughter die in her eyes, replaced by fury. A smile tugged at the corner of his mouth. She wasn't as unaffected by him as she pretended to be. He tore his eyes from the gorgeous woman fuming at the other end of the arena as the cowboy manning the gate let him through.

Focusing on the steer in the chute, he backed his mare inside and eased her to the rear of the box. He could feel her muscles twitching with anticipation and felt a moment of satisfaction at the mare's abilities. She loved her job, loved the burst of speed as she kept the steer lined up and running straight, and was a natural for the sport. He looked at the cowboy in the box, waiting for his nod signaling the man at the chute to loose the steer.

Both cowboys came out of the box simultaneously, and Clay watched as his partner leaned off his horse, his hand sliding up the side of the steer's neck to curl around the right horn as his left hand pulled the other one down, turning the steer's head toward his armpit. The cowboy's horse continued forward without him as he slipped his feet from the stirrups and dug his heels into the soft dirt, wrapping his hand around the steer's muzzle and curling its head so that their momentum carried them both to the ground. Clay watched over his shoulder, slowing his mare as he retrieved his partner's gelding from where he had stopped and stood patiently waiting.

As they exited the arena, he led the steer wrestler's horse back to the arena entrance, preparing to make the run again, this time with a young, first-time bulldogger. He knew the kid wouldn't be in the money, but everyone needed to start somewhere, and he wanted to help him out.

He caught a blur of a black and white paint horse coming around from behind him, and his heart pounded painfully against his chest before kicking into high gear.

When he realized it was Scott, riding his own horse again, he couldn't help but feel a flood of disappointment. Clay clenched his jaw at the reaction. He was *not* looking for Jennifer. He didn't want to talk to her or watch her ride or remember how soft her lips were against his. Coming to this rodeo had been a bad idea, he thought to himself for the hundredth time already.

"CLAY!" HE TURNED around and saw Mike riding toward him on the ugliest sorrel he'd ever seen. He remembered Digger. Every cowboy loved the gelding. He was the ugliest beast on the ranch but also the most trustworthy; the crew fought to use him for rodeos when the boss wasn't riding him. "A little bird told me you were here."

Clay dropped his grooming supplies into the tack compartment of the trailer and shoved the saddle onto the rack. "Scott?"

"Jennifer," Mike corrected.

Clay couldn't help arching his eyebrow, surprised that Jennifer had even acknowledged his presence, let alone mentioned his name. "I thought my ears were burning."

"I made her put the voodoo doll away," Mike joked. "Heading back out already?"

"Oregon's a long drive," Clay replied.

"Don't rush off. Stay and have dinner with us."

The old man had been like a father to Clay, which he'd always appreciated since his own father had run off when he was just a kid. It hadn't been easy growing up with few male role models, watching his mother skip from bed to bed trying to find a man to take care of her. She'd only ended up with heartbreak, too many mouths to feed, and several unhealthy addictions. Clay had been fortunate enough to earn a scholarship to a college as far away as he could get at seventeen. He had been lucky to get away and even luckier to land the job with Findley Brothers, as inexperienced as he'd been.

About as lucky as you were to have Jen fall in love with you. But you ruined that, too, you idiot.

"I don't think everyone will be as happy to see me as you are, Mike."

The old man crossed his wrists over the saddle horn, his reins dangling in his fingers, and laughed. "Jennifer's not going to do anything. You know better than anyone, she's all bark and no bite."

Clay glanced warily toward the Findley Brothers' trailers. Even though he hoped to catch another glimpse of her, he knew it was best to avoid her. "I don't think it's a good idea, Mike. I mean, what if—"

"I have a proposition for you, Clay," he interrupted. "I need your help. One of my guys just had to bail, personal reasons, and I can't find someone else on this short of notice. We have a rodeo next weekend, and I really need someone with experience or we'll have to cancel."

"What about Derek?"

Mike cocked his head to the side. "I love that boy, but we both know Derek is *not* a pickup man. At least, he won't be anytime soon. He has a lot of growing up to do before I want to put him in charge of saving lives."

"I haven't talked to him since I left, so I can't say." Clay didn't want to point out that Derek was simply coddled by everyone at the ranch and needed to stand on his own feet for a bit. He'd cowboy up if anyone ever gave him the opportunity. But it wasn't his place to say anything. He'd given up that right when he walked out on Jen and the rest of the family.

"Mike, I have to get back to Oregon. I have a job there, remember?" He knew he was making excuses and was sure Mike did, too.

Mike sat up in the saddle, sighing heavily, and shook his head. "Okay, I just thought that since you skipped out on me once before, you'd want to make it up to a feeble old man."

Clay laughed out loud. "Feeble, you? When did you start dishing out guilt trips?"

"About the same time you decided to leave me in a lurch five years ago." His eyes twinkled with merriment, as if he knew Clay was about to give in. Mike never minced words, but he didn't seem to hold Clay's departure against him. Clay knew he couldn't say no, not after all Mike had done for him in the past.

"Fine. I'll let them know I won't be back until next week. They don't have anything on the schedule for a while." Clay narrowed his eyes as Mike grinned like the proverbial Cheshire Cat. "I'm only going to this one rodeo, Mike."

"One rodeo, got it."

Why did Clay get the feeling he'd just sold his soul to the devil?

JENNIFER BROUGHT THE sausages to Scott at the barbecue pit and sighed. She felt weary, but she wasn't sure if it was because of the stress from traveling, not sleeping because of her nightmares, or Clay showing up at the rodeo today. Her eyes slid across the near-empty parking lot where most of the crew congregated, waiting for dinner, and saw Derek laughing with Clay by one of the trailers.

"What is he still doing here?" she muttered. It irritated her that everyone seemed to accept his presence as if he'd never left.

The corner of Scott's mouth quirked. "He said Mike asked him to stay to help with the rodeo next weekend." He slid the plate of sausages from her hands like he didn't trust her not to throw them.

"He did what?" Mike knew what a low-down, conniving, back-stabbing jackass Clay was. Why would he possibly ask him to come back, even for a weekend? "He wouldn't do that."

"He did. Jake's dad is sick, and it looks like he'll be in the hospital for at least a week. Mike told him to go be with his dad as long as he needs to." She could see the empathy in Scott's eyes. They understood the pain of losing a parent, and none of them would ever begrudge someone time with family. Even if it meant she had to face Clay for a week.

"Is he going to be all right?"

Scott chewed at the corner of his mouth. "Don't know."

"I'll call and see how he's doing tonight." Jen looked back where Clay was now laughing with several of the crew. She wondered if she could manage to just ignore him until after the next rodeo. He had changed a lot in the past few years, filling out in all the right places. But his green eyes were somber, even more so than when he'd first come to work for Mike at the ranch. There had always been a quiet melancholy that hung over Clay, and he refused to open up about his past. Whenever she asked, he would grow silent before changing the subject, always reminding her how grateful he was for her love.

Now, he had a determined set to his chiseled jaw, and when his full lips spread to laugh, a dimple creased his left cheek. She'd always loved his smile. Her eyes flicked up, and she realized he was watching her appraising him. She looked away quickly, hoping he wouldn't assume her evaluation was any indication of attraction. That was the last thing she would ever feel for Clay Graham again. She might be a lot of things, but a fool wasn't one of them.

She headed for her trailer to prepare a pitcher of tea, refusing to give any credence to the idea that she might be retreating into the one place she knew Clay wouldn't be brave enough to enter. She ignored the flutters in her belly at the thought of him staying for a week. Damn Mike for asking him to stay, and damn Clay for accepting the offer. She stirred the sugar into the tea with a vengeance borne out of anger before bumping the screen door open with her hip and stepping onto the metal stairs.

"Here, let me help."

She jumped at the sound of Clay's voice, tripping down the last step, nearly falling in the short grass, and spilling tea over the side of the pitcher onto her hand. Clay's hands found her waist, catching her, and heat sizzled down her sides, making her heart race and pooling in her stomach before traveling lower. She quickly stepped away from him, leaving him with his hands suspended in the air for a moment, as if he didn't know how to react to her escape. Clay dropped his hands against his thighs and sighed, staring at her as if her reaction disappointed him.

"I can manage on my own." She looked away, drying her hand on her jeans. Unable to miss the sharp, icy note in her own voice, she wished she could have faked ambivalence instead. "I've been doing it for a long time without you."

Way to make him think you're over him, Jen.

Clay bit his lower lip, taking a deep breath through his nose, controlling himself. She remembered how he used to do it whenever he got angry. What did *he* have to be angry about?

He let out the breath slowly, weighing his words. "I know you have." His voice was husky and deep, like the Scotch Mike had given her to dull the pain after she'd realized he wasn't coming back, after he'd apologized to everyone but her. "Jen, I'm sorry I left the way I did. I should have at least called you."

"You think?" The words were jagged and calloused, the way her heart felt. "You left me sleeping with your ring on my finger the day after giving it to me. Why did you even bother asking? And to think, your apology only took five years to make. Glad I didn't hold my breath waiting for it."

She spun to leave, but he reached for her elbow, pulling her back toward him. "I didn't mean to hurt you, Jen."

Of all the things she'd expected to hear from him, of all the excuses she imagined over the years, this was the most asinine thing he could have said. With nearly five years to think of something, anything, to say, this was the best he could manage? She couldn't help the acrimonious laughter that spilled out.

"You asked me to spend the rest of my life with you and then disappeared in the middle of the night without so much as a good-bye. Then you called and apologize to my family, not me but *my family*, and now you say you didn't mean to *hurt* me? What did you think it would do?"

He ran his free hand over his face, looking haggard and sorrowful. "I don't know. I was a stupid kid. It was five years ago. I didn't know how to tell you I was scared."

"You were scared?" She jerked her elbow from his fingers. "Did you ever stop to think *I* might be scared too? But when you love someone, you work through the fear. I loved you enough to muddle through it and face the fear *with* you. Apparently, I was the only one."

"That hasn't been my experience with love. I've seen too much go wrong, seen love fail every time. And that wasn't what I was afraid of, Jen. With my past—"

"I don't know your past, Clay." She could feel her heart softening, wanting to give in to him, to forgive him. She'd loved this man once, with every beat of her heart, but it hadn't been enough. "You wouldn't open up to me. You never did."

She wanted to see the sadness disappear from his eyes the way it used to when they were together, to let him hold her the way he used to, the two of them shutting out the world. Her heart beat painfully against her ribs. Giving in to him and watching him walk away again would kill her. The first time had taught her the foolishness of allowing someone into every recess of her heart. She wasn't stupid enough to do it twice.

"You had your chance and you threw it away. It's going to take more than a lame excuse for me to forgive you." She spun on her heel, leaving him and their past behind her.

CLAY FOLLOWED JEN'S every move with his eyes, barely listening to Scott. Jen rose and threw her paper plate and plastic utensils in the garbage bag tied to the end of the table. She had no idea how graceful she looked, even doing menial tasks, or how much he had missed watching her over the past few years. Years of staring at the picture he'd kept in his wallet hadn't done justice to seeing the living, breathing woman in front of him now. She had an easy, understated elegance about her. Something about the way she made riding any horse look effortless and the way she seemed to glide as she walked. Every movement was fluid, like she was dancing. He couldn't help but remember how she looked lost in the throes of passion.

Better stop now, Clay, because if she knew what you were thinking about, she'd kill you right here in front of everyone.

His body seemed determined to defy his brain. No woman should look the way she did. With her hair pulled through the back of a baseball cap, she was the picture of innocence. Everything about her was modest, as if she were trying to hide her beauty, but any man could see it. She was barefaced, as always after a rodeo, but she had never needed any sort of makeup. Her dark lashes surrounded eyes so deep brown that they were almost black. Her olive skin tone was highlighted by a tan from spending so much time outdoors. Her golden brown ponytail hung in loose waves almost to her waist, longer than he remembered, and he itched to run his fingers through her hair. He wanted to slide his fingers over the indentation at her waist and the gentle flare of her hips. The last five years had been kind to her, turning her coltish frame into womanly curves.

"You're a glutton for punishment, Clay." Scott pointed out the obvious.

Clay tore his eyes from Jen as she entered her trailer. "What makes you say that?"

"You know she hates you, right? She'd rather shoot you than forgive you."

He knew Scott was joking, sort of, but his heart clenched anyway. It killed him knowing how badly he'd hurt her when he'd left, but after their earlier conversation, he didn't think she really hated him. In fact, he wondered if her hurt wasn't the main reason for her anger.

Clay rolled his eyes and gave Scott a confident grin. He was starting to formulate a plan for the next week. "Only because she needs a little persuasion." He let his gaze linger on her as she came out with another pitcher of iced tea.

"You obviously don't remember how my sister can hold a grudge."

"You obviously don't remember how charismatic I am."

Scott snorted a laugh. "Yeah, I think that ship has sailed already."

Clay eyed his friend, praying he was wrong, even as he contemplated walking away from this entire mess again. He was sure Mike could find another pickup man for the rodeo next week, but he had a feeling Mike was trying to play matchmaker. The only thing he wanted was to get Jen's forgiveness and then to move on with a clear conscience, something that was long overdue.

"Ten bucks says I can make her smile."

"Twenty bucks says you don't."

"Thirty bucks says she slaps you and walks away." Both men looked over to see Derek flop down into one of the folding chairs.

"Thanks for the vote of confidence," Clay muttered, rising to his feet and grabbing their empty plates. The thought of Jen hating him forever was more than he could bear, and he was going to do his best to remedy the situation.

"Good luck," Scott called after him.

"You'll need it," Derek added.

"Mind if I get a refill?"

Jennifer rolled her eyes at Clay but slid the pitcher toward him. "Be my guest." She turned to leave. The less time she spent near him, the easier it would be to get through the next week.

"Do you realize everyone is making bets on how long it will take before you slap me?"

She arched a brow at him and leaned her hip against the table. "Really? Who has five minutes?"

"I think that would be me." A smile curved his lips. It made him look younger and less cynical. He was always so damn handsome when he smiled.

She forced herself to look away, busying herself with shifting the food on the table and stacking empty bowls. "Then I'll wait a few more minutes so someone I like wins the money." She gripped the edge of a half-empty bowl of potato salad.

He tried to hide the frown that furrowed his brow and turned his lips down again. It only lasted a second before he grinned and shot a glance at her brothers, still seated near Mike's trailer. "Come on, Jen. How can you say you don't like me?" He moved a step closer to her, his fingers toying at the side of the bowl, over hers.

Her gaze bounced from their hands to his green eyes. "It's real easy. I. Don't. Like. You." She made sure to enunciate every word. Why couldn't he get the hint? She didn't want anything to do with him, not now, not ever again.

Jen pulled her hand from under his, but he took a step closer, his gaze holding her own. "You used to be friendlier," he pointed out.

"And *you* used to be charming."

Clay straightened his shoulders and took another step toward her as she backed away. "I'm still charming, with people who aren't antagonistic."

How dare he insinuate that *she* was being antagonistic? Okay, well, maybe she was, but he deserved every bit of resentment she directed at him. The man left her lying in his bed after proposing and never gave her any explanation for his departure. She narrowed her eyes for a moment before she allowed a sweet smile to curve her lips.

"I'm so sorry, Clay. I didn't mean to be so hostile." She reached again for the potato salad. "You're right, I used to be friendlier. Let's start again. I'm Jen," she said, thrusting her right hand out.

He eyed her suspiciously but took the bait, curling his fingers around her hand. "I'm Clay. Jen, do you realize you have the most amazing eyes?" He flirted with her.

"Thank you." She gave him her most engaging smile and leaned toward him. "Tell me, Clay, who had the bet that I'd dump potato salad on your head?"

"What?"

He barely opened his mouth before she upended the plastic bowl over him. Bits of mayonnaise, carrots, and potatoes dripped down his face, and she couldn't stop herself from laughing out loud as she quickly moved from his reach. Clay swiped at the mess on his face, flinging it from his hands to the ground. She heard the laughter from her brothers behind her and looked over at them.

"Next time, don't make bets about me." She shoved the bowl into Clay's chest. "And the three of you can clean up this mess. I'm leaving."

Chapter Three

CLAY WATCHED HER walk away through the haze of mayo and potatoes, trying not to admire the sway of her hips and the way her jeans curved along her perfectly round bottom. Damn, but that woman was full of piss and vinegar. He should have known better than to fall for that sweet, honeyed tone. It lured him in every time, even when they were younger and she'd pulled a prank on him with her brothers' help. Every time Jen turned those dark eyes on him, it was like his brain took a semipermanent vacation. He plucked a piece of potato from behind his ear and flung it to the ground.

"That's a good look on you." Scott laughed as he passed Clay a few bills.

Clay glared at him. "What's this?"

"The bet was that you could make her smile. You actually made her laugh, so I'd say you won, fair and square."

Derek held out his money. "Although I don't think this was what you had planned, Mr. Charismatic."

Clay snatched the money out of their hands and tucked the bills into his pocket. "You guys help me clean this up, and I'll buy you drinks tonight." He saw Derek's eyes light up. "Not you, Ace. You may look like a man, but I'm not contributing to the delinquency of a minor. Besides, your sister would have my ass if she found out I gave you a beer."

He looked over as he heard one of the trucks start up and saw Jen pull out of the parking area.

"Come on, Clay. She won't even be here," Derek complained.

"Where does she think she's going?"

Scott shrugged. "Not sure, but she looked pissed. Maybe you should get cleaned up and go after her."

"Are you nuts?" Clay glared at Scott. "I'm not going after that woman. She's insane." He headed for Mike's trailer as Scott followed him.

"Well, someone's got to go. And who do you think made her this way, Clay? It certainly wasn't us."

Clay reached for the hose on the outside of the trailer and twisted the knob, letting the icy water run over his head as it rinsed white globs of potato onto the dirt, splattering his boots. Scott was right. He was the one who turned Jen into this sarcastic shell of the sweet, trusting woman she'd been. She might be even sexier than she'd been before, but he'd destroyed her blind faith in others when he'd abandoned her. He had to make her understand why he'd done it, at least offer her his weak explanation, whether or not she forgave him. He owed her that much, even if it left him exposed.

"Fine, I'll go after her. Lend me a truck since my rig is still hooked up."

Scott slapped a set of keys into his hand. "You better not leave my truck smelling like potato salad."

THANK GOODNESS FOR cell phones, Clay thought. Until Jen finally answered Derek's call, Clay had no idea where to even start looking for her. The last place he'd expected to find her was the local bar. He parked Scott's truck in the first empty spot he could find, three doors down from what looked like a very rowdy bar with a questionable crowd. He wasn't one to prejudge, but the motorcycles parked out front didn't bode well, particularly for someone wearing boots and a cowboy hat. Clay opened the front door and slipped into the dark entrance, letting his eyes adjust from the blazing sunset outside to the neon lit interior of the bar. He scanned the tables for Jen but didn't see her.

Laughter at the bar immediately caught his attention. He'd know that laugh anywhere. It haunted every dream he'd ever had about her. He clenched his jaw when he realized he hadn't seen Jen at first because she was surrounded by no less than five bikers, all vying for her attention. Clay's gut twisted. He was suddenly certain there was a high probability he was going to get into a fight tonight, and it was unlikely he'd come out on the winning side. He had to be smart about this if he wanted to get out with his face intact.

"Hey hon," he called, making his way between the men before they realized what was happening. "You already ordered for us? The rest of the boys are parking the trucks. Come dance with me," Clay spit the words out quickly, leaving no room to argue or protest.

He slipped his hand around Jen's, pulling her from the bar stool and onto her feet. He dragged her toward the jukebox in the corner and dropped several coins in, punching random buttons.

Jen's mouth dropped open in surprise, but for the first time, she looked at a loss for words. He wrapped his arm around her waist and pulled her close as a slow Two-Step filled the speakers. Clay inhaled the scent of her as he leaned down to whisper into her ear, hating the way his body instantly responded to her curves pressed against him.

"Don't argue, don't fight, and go along with anything I say," he said in a low growl, irritated that he even had to come up with this ruse to try to get them both out without any trouble.

She glared at him. "How did you even know I was here?"

"Derek."

"Traitor," she muttered. "Well, as you can see, I'm fine, and I don't need your assistance."

"Who's driving you back, Miss Independent? I'm sure you aren't in any condition to drive." Clay tried to ignore how good she felt in his arms, how right, how much he wanted to kiss her smart mouth until she stopped arguing with him.

She glanced back at the bar where several of the bikers were still paying too much attention to them and gave a little wave. "I'm sure any one of those guys would take me home."

"I'm sure you're right," he said through gritted teeth. "But I don't think your home is where they'd take you." He eased her toward the front door, sliding his hand into his pocket and curling his fingers around Scott's keys. "We're leaving. Go right to Scott's truck and start it up. Now." He pressed the keys into her hand. "If you want us both out of here in one piece, go now!" His voice became insistent when she didn't move toward the door.

"Hey!"

He heard the biker yell before he saw him headed their way. The bartender turned away, ignoring the fight they all knew was coming. It didn't take long for several others to follow the first biker over. Clay shoved Jen out the front door and turned, determined to distract them and give her a few minutes head start.

Holding his hands in the air, he tried to look as apologetic as possible. "Sorry, man, but my wife sometimes gets a little out of hand. We haven't been married long, and you know how some women just don't realize they need to stay home."

The group stopped short, eyeing Clay suspiciously. "She's your old lady?" the first biker asked.

"Yeah." Clay said with a sigh as he tried to edge closer to the door and his escape.

"You need to keep that one on a leash, cowboy." The bikers laughed but were looking confused, and Clay took advantage of the moment.

"Don't I know it!" He slid his hand into his pocket and drew out the bills from Scott and Derek. "Why don't you guys have a few drinks on me, to make up for any inconvenience she might have caused?"

The biker closest to Clay, one of the largest in the bunch, eyed several of the others before plucking the money from Clay's fingers. "You'd better get your old lady home, man, before that pretty little thing gets you in any more trouble."

Clay wasn't about to test his good luck. He nodded at the biker before pushing open the door. He walked out just in time to see Jen drop Scott's truck into gear and start to pull out of the parking spot. Was she planning on leaving him here to deal with those guys? He ran in front of the truck and slammed his hand onto the hood, startling her while she looked over her shoulder to back out.

"Where the hell do you think you're going?"

"Anywhere you aren't!" she yelled back.

"Get in the passenger seat, Jen. You are *not* driving this truck drunk." He was trying his best to keep his voice calm and reasonable when every fiber of his being wanted to throttle her.

"I'm not drunk, you idiot. If you hadn't played the macho hero, I'd be driving my own truck back."

Clay reached his hand through the rolled down driver's side window and pushed the button to unlock the door. He yanked it open as several bikers came outside to witness the commotion and his humiliation. A few started snickering, laughing about how he couldn't control his woman. And then the catcalls came.

"Looks like the little firecracker's got his number!"

"Hey, cowboy, maybe you should stick to horses and leave the lady for a real man."

He climbed inside the truck, forcing her to unbuckle her seat belt and slide over, before slamming the door behind him.

"Don't shove me!"

Turning to face her, he inhaled deeply, trying to control the rage pulsing through his veins. Her eyes were wide, as wild as he was sure his were at that moment, her lips parted, and he realized that a few years ago, they would have settled this argument without clothing. It would have been a passionate, fiery explosion of need and want and desire. And love.

The thought doused his anger like a bucket of cold water.

At one time, Jen had given him everything, willingly. She'd offered him every ounce of her mind, body, and soul, keeping nothing back for herself. And he'd thrown it away like an old blanket. For a man who'd spent his youth wanting someone to love him for who he was, to accept him and never turn their back on him, he'd sure crapped on the one person who'd done just that. Clay gripped the steering wheel, twisting his hands against the leather cover before dropping his forehead against his knuckles. The anger was long gone, leaving sorrow and regret in its wake. He punched the button to roll up the window, unable to look at her.

"I'm sorry, Jen. God, you have no idea how sorry I am."

He felt, rather than saw, her edge farther toward the passenger door, farther from him, from what they'd once had. "I don't care if you're sorry."

Her voice was cold, emotionless, and he sought her eyes to see if she was lying. She stared out the passenger window, refusing to look at him, but he thought he saw her swipe at her cheek. Was she crying? Jen never cried, and he couldn't imagine she'd have any tears for him after what he'd done. He wanted to ask for her forgiveness, to know if her tears were for what they'd lost or because it had ever been. Instead he retreated, too afraid to hear the truth. He might not blame her for hating him, but he didn't want to hear her say it.

JENNIFER STARED OUT the window, refusing to look at the obnoxious man beside her. How dare he come and escort her from the bar like she was an irresponsible kid. He wasn't her boss and he wasn't her father. He certainly wasn't her husband, and he had no right to tell people he was. She wiped her cheek, praying he didn't see the angry tears.

She hadn't cried over him in years, even if he had crossed her mind every single day since he left. She tried to convince herself that the only reason she'd thought about him over the past few years was to remind herself what a fool she'd been to buy into his country boy charm and lies. He was a cowboy all right, and he'd saddled up and moved on without her, no matter what promise he'd made. Scott and Derek trusted him; Mike adored him. She wasn't going to let him make a fool of them either, even if it meant making sure she protected her family from his desertion this time around. They might not see it, but she wasn't blind.

As they pulled through the gates of the rodeo grounds, Clay parked the truck just off of the driveway. "We need to talk."

"I have nothing to say to you." She wouldn't look at him, even as her heart begged her to turn his way, to lose herself in those green eyes.

"Jen, please. Don't make this any more difficult than it already is."

His voice was gentle, coaxing, holding a pleading note she'd only heard from him once before, in a solitary moment of vulnerability just before he proposed. She tried to remind herself he'd lied then and would lie now, too, but her heart wouldn't listen. She hated the desire she felt to comfort him. She turned her head toward him slightly, giving him only a view of her profile.

"I hurt you. I get it. I really do. I don't blame you for feeling the way you do but—"

He paused, running his hand through his hair. She hadn't seen it this long before, nearly hanging into his eyes. Her fingers itched to brush the locks back from his forehead.

"I don't even know what else to say. I can't make this better." Clay shook his head in defeat.

"It will never be the same, Clay. I'm not the same. I don't want to be." She couldn't look directly at him, didn't want to acknowledge the very real hurt that flickered over his face at her declaration. She turned back toward the window.

"Can you at least give me a chance to explain?"

"What's to explain, Clay? You asked me to marry you, we celebrated with my entire family, and then you ran out a few hours later. I'd say it was all pretty self-explanatory." She didn't want to talk about any of this with him. He hadn't bothered to call her in five years, hadn't felt the need to offer any excuses before—why did he suddenly want to explain everything? She grabbed her purse and flung open the door, heading toward the trailers in the back, her boots kicking up dust.

"Dammit, Jennifer!" She heard the truck door slam as he ran after her. "Will you stop for two seconds and just listen? You don't have this all figured out, no matter what you think."

Clay grabbed her arm, and she spun on him, wildly swinging her purse at his head and jerking her arm from his grasp. "Don't touch me."

He easily caught the purse in his hand and dropped it at his feet as he pulled her into his arms. "What do you have in that thing? Bricks?"

"Let go of me, Clay," she said through gritted teeth, twisting, trying to release herself from his grasp.

"Only if you let me explain."

Every inch of her that was in contact with him burned with icy flames. The heat of his hands on her arms sent warmth running down her spine to melt her limbs and ignite the desire pooling in her belly. She wanted to push him away, to run to her trailer and stay there until he went back to wherever he'd been hiding, but when her eyes met his, pleading with her to listen to him, she couldn't deny herself just one more moment with him. How was she supposed to keep hating him when her body wouldn't follow her commands?

"You have five minutes." One for each year she hadn't heard from him. He released her cautiously. She walked back to the truck, knowing he would follow, and flipped the tailgate down. She hopped up on it, letting her legs dangle. When he sighed and scrubbed a hand over his jaw, she quirked a brow. "Time's ticking Clay. Start talking."

"You know, for someone who seems to think she has everything figured out better than the rest of us, you sure can be irresponsible. What were you thinking going into that bar?"

Jen almost let her mouth fall open at the audacity of his accusation. She bit the inside of her cheek until the metallic taste of blood forced her to stop.

She jumped from the back of the truck. "That was some explanation. I can't believe I waited this long for it."

Clay's fingers circled her wrist as she started to walk away. "I have at least three minutes left."

He pulled her back toward him, drawing her against his chest as one arm circled around her waist. His other hand buried into her long hair, and she gasped in surprise as his mouth found hers. Her body betrayed her again, melting against him as her bones seemed to turn to molten lava. Her fingers dug into the muscles of his shoulders, but she wasn't sure if it was to keep her balance or because she couldn't resist touching him. His mouth was gentle, in spite of their argument, as if he wanted to savor this kiss, to taste her, to force the memories of the tenderness they'd once shared to the surface. Clay nipped at her lower lip, testing her resolve, and when she didn't protest, he plunged ahead. His tongue swept against hers as she slid her hands over his shoulders before curling her fingers around the nape of his neck, twining into his hair.

Clay's lips trailed over her cheek and jaw. "I've missed you, Jen. You have no idea how much."

The reality of their situation hit her. What in the hell was she doing? This was the same man who'd walked away and left her with nothing more than a diamond solitaire encircling the broken shards of her heart, all without so much as a backward glance. How could she have forgotten the pain, the agony, as the years passed without even a call to break the silence? She shoved him away and reached into her pocket.

"I could tell from all the phone calls, letters, and messages you sent over the past five years." She saw his eyes cloud with frustration. She stared down at the ring glinting between her thumb and forefinger.

"When you left, I thought I was going to die. I loved you Clay. I loved you more than I ever thought it was possible for me to love anyone. And you showed me that none of that mattered. You threw it all away. You still haven't told me why." She held the ring out to him. "I want you to leave again. Disappear. But this time, don't come back."

She slapped the ring into his hand and turned on her heel, walking away before he could say anything.

SHE WAS HAPPY he didn't follow her. *She was.* But if that were true, then why did she keep checking over her shoulder? Why was it hard to breathe? Why did her heart ache as painfully as it did the last time he turned his back on her?

Things had always been explosive between them, too often like a wildfire, out of control. They fought passionately, but they loved just as a fiercely—at least that was what she'd thought. She pushed the memory of Clay's lips on hers away with near physical force. How could she have been stupid enough to let him kiss her like that? What the hell was he doing back here, and why was he bent on ripping her heart out again?

She slammed the door of her trailer and locked it. She needed some privacy and didn't want either of her brothers coming to check up on her. *Traitors.* She'd ignored several of their phone calls at the bar before finally checking in so they wouldn't worry about her hasty retreat, and Derek had given her up. What possessed him to send Clay after her? Well, that mistake would earn him a night sleeping in the seat of the pickup, the jerk.

She looked around the trailer for something, anything that might distract her. She reached for a glass and filled it with iced tea from the pitcher inside the refrigerator. She wasn't thirsty, the three glasses of club soda with lime at the bar had quenched any thirst, but she couldn't sit still.

She shook her head as she remembered Clay, charging into the bar, prepared to fight with the bikers because he thought she'd been too drunk to take care of herself. She didn't need his bravado. She'd been stone-cold sober. Like she'd ever have driven drunk after what happened to her parents. Now she had to find time tomorrow to go get her truck. The fact that he thought he could come riding back into her life, five years after leaving, and tell her what to do infuriated her. She inhaled deeply, trying to control her anger. Clay Graham could find some other damsel in distress to rescue because she had no use for him in his tarnished armor. She'd been taking care of herself and her brothers since she was in a training bra; she didn't need his help now.

She set the glass onto the counter and went into the bedroom, pulling out a pair of yoga pants and a T-shirt, tossing them onto the bed before climbing into the shower. Maybe the hot water would wash away the frustration curling in her chest. It was bad enough that she was going to be forced to face Clay again tomorrow. She didn't want to deal with his presence at the ranch for the next week. She lathered her hair and sighed in defeat. At least back at the ranch, she could busy herself with the animals and avoid him.

Just one more day and you can head home.

Jennifer deeply inhaled the scent of coconuts and vanilla. It made her think of suntan lotion and sunny beaches. Maybe she just needed a vacation. Some place to sip piña coladas and relax while the ocean tickled her toes.

Sure, at the start of rodeo season. You might as well plan on taking a rowboat to the moon.

Her family needed her, and she wouldn't let them down. Not now or ever. Mike had done more than any man could be expected to do for his best friend's kids— he'd taken them in as his own and had taken Scott's side over his daughter's false accusations. In spite of Scott and Derek's most recent lapse of judgment, she knew they only had her best interests in mind. They would both do anything for her, the way she would for them. They were a tight family, and she wasn't about to let anything, or anyone, break that bond.

The banging on the front door jerked her from her thoughts, making her jump in surprise and nearly fall, her foot sliding in the conditioner on the shower floor. "I'm coming," she yelled. "Derek, just hang on."

Quickly rinsing her hair, she threw on clothes and wrapped a towel around her head before flipping the lock on the door and heading back to the bedroom. "I should make you sleep in the horse trailer after what you pulled today." She dropped the wet towel onto the bed and reached for her comb.

"It wouldn't be the first time."

Jennifer spun at the sound of Clay's voice, the wet strands of her long hair slapping against her face and sticking to her cheeks. "What are you doing in here?"

His green eyes glinted with humor, but that wasn't all she saw there. She refused to put a name to what she thought she recognized. "Well, you didn't exactly let me finish explaining."

"And you weren't exactly talking," she countered. "Look, Clay, I'm tired, and I don't feel like fighting with you. I just want to go to bed."

"If you say so." A slow, seductive smile spread over his full lips. He sat on the couch and pushed the toe of his boot against the heel of the other foot, repeating the motion with the opposite boot, then he stood and unbuckled his belt.

She glared at him, hoping he would get the hint that she wasn't in the mood for his childish games. "I seem to recall you couldn't get *out* of my bed fast enough. You're no longer welcome." She turned and headed back for the bedroom door, reaching for her comb. "I assume you know the way out. You didn't seem to have trouble finding it last time." It was a low blow, but when it came to Clay, her mouth seemed to operate without permission from her heart.

He moved silently to the bedroom and watched her brush out her hair. It made her self-conscious, and she jerked at the tresses, in a hurry to get away from his prying gaze. She glanced up to see him leaning against the doorframe, his eyes dark with the same yearning that was pulsing through her veins. Even now, in the face of his desertion, he made her breath catch and the blood pound like a bass drum, creating a swirling need that centered in her chest, beating against the walls of her heart.

Only Clay had ever made her feel this way. From the first time those green eyes met hers across the corral at the ranch, his heated gaze had a way of making her insides burn, while her skin tingled with anticipation of his touch. Damn him.

Her hands trembled, and she dropped her comb on the floor. *Way to look like he doesn't have you tied in knots, Jennifer.*

He covered the distance between them, retrieving her comb. "Sit," he ordered, pressing on her shoulder so she sat at the foot of the bed. Clay's hand slid under her hair, grazing the base of her neck, causing a shiver of delightful tingles to travel down the length of her spine. He closed his fist around her hair and carefully combed the snarls from the lower half. Once he finished, he released his grip and worked the comb from her roots to the ends. She bit back a sigh of bliss at his touch. Each stroke ignited sparks of need, miniature explosions of longing throughout her body. He rested his free hand on her shoulder, his fingers finding the curve of her neck. It was such a tender caress; she closed her eyes, allowing herself a moment of pure joy, a few seconds to imagine they were younger, in another time, before mistakes were made and hearts were broken.

Just the thought brought her back to the present, and her head fell forward, her chin dropping to her chest. She sighed. "Why did you come here?" she whispered.

He didn't speak for a long time, and she began to wonder if he had even heard her question. "I just wanted to apologize."

Nothing more. He only wanted to assuage his guilt. The painful truth of his answer was nearly her undoing, as her heart made its own confession—she still loved him. He'd left her with her heart broken, bleeding, and betrayed, and she couldn't deny she still had feelings for him, but they simply weren't returned. She might want him; she just didn't want the pain that came with loving him. And she couldn't allow herself to fall prey again.

"I don't want you to," she lied. "I will never forgive you for what you did."

"I was protecting you."

"No." Jennifer rose and took the comb from his hand, careful not to touch him. "You were protecting yourself." She walked to the trailer door and opened it. "Please, leave."

Chapter Four

CLAY HAD JUST dropped into one of the folding chairs outside Scott's trailer when Scott joined him. "Trouble?"

He could see the humor in his friend's eyes and thought about punching him for a brief moment. "Shut up." He dropped his head back and stared up at the stars. "What was I thinking?"

"Well, I guess that really depends on when you mean," Scott said. "Now, or when you first left?"

Clay shrugged, not really expecting an answer to his rhetorical question.

"If the question doesn't matter, Clay, then neither does the answer."

He shot Scott a sideways glare. "Sounds like you've been hanging around Mike too long."

"Okay, here's a better question—are you happy with the way things have turned out since you left?"

"I don't know," Clay confessed. "I thought leaving would be the best way to protect her. In a way it did, but in some ways, it did the opposite. I couldn't be two places at the same time." He saw Scott looking at him skeptically and defended himself. "My brother had just been found dead. My mom needed my help."

"You ran away and never even called her. Face it, you were scared."

"I was twenty-two years old. I wasn't ready for a pre-made family. I didn't even know how to take care of myself, let alone support your sister and both of you."

Scott sat up in his chair and leaned forward. "Who are you trying to kid? Jen never expected you to support her or us. We've been working with Mike since our parents died, and we all know this is a *family* business. We do it together." The light above the door highlighted the muscle ticking in Scott's jaw as he narrowed his eyes. "She never asked you to step in and be our father. Matter of fact, she never asked you for anything, but she offered you everything. You were just too chicken to accept it, and so you crawled back into that pit you thought you were destined for."

Scott stood and shook his head. "I don't know what kind of bullshit you've been telling yourself over the past five years, but the Clay I remember would have at least been honest. You might have left to help your mom, but you stayed away because you were too scared to admit the truth to Jen."

He just walked away without giving Clay a chance to respond, leaving Clay staring at his empty hands, wondering how he could have ever imagined what he had now was worth what he'd given up.

JENNIFER SLID OPEN the door between her room and the kitchenette of the trailer and saw Clay sleeping in Derek's spot on the couch, a thin throw blanket twisted around his legs. Typical cowboy, sleeping in whatever he was wearing and wherever he dropped. She tried not to stare at the broad wall of muscle that made up his chest or the way his T-shirt had ridden up, giving her a clear view of the ridges of his abs just above his belt buckle. She bit her lip and reached for a coffee cup, her mouth practically watering over the sexy specimen of male perfection lying on her couch. Clay had always been good looking, but the last few years had been generous to his physique. She didn't want to begin wondering about how the last five years had affected him emotionally. She knew how it had changed her and delving into that conversation would light a powder keg of vulnerability she wasn't sure she could handle.

Clay had never been one to share his feelings. Hell, he'd barely shared his *thoughts* when they'd been dating. Nor did he seem inclined to offer anything to her now other than an apology for leaving. She didn't want to hear his excuses; she wanted to know the truth. What had been so much more valuable to him than their relationship, than her heart? He stirred enough to shift on the small couch, trying to find some measure of comfort. His T-shirt rode higher on his side as he threw an arm over his head, smacking his knuckles against the wall.

"Ow." He checked his hand for damage. She couldn't help but smile as she poured water into the small coffee pot on the counter, forcing herself to tear her eyes away from him.

"You could have let me sleep a bit longer," he muttered.

"You want to work with Mike, you know the rules. Up early and animals first." She watched as he sat up and scrubbed a hand over the scruff of beard growth on his jaw. "Coffee will be ready in a few minutes."

Clay eyed her suspiciously. "You're sort of friendly this morning."

"Yeah? Well, probably because you haven't pissed me off yet. But I'm sure you'll remedy that before breakfast."

Clay rose and made his way toward her in stocking feet. She wanted to back away from him but forced herself to stand her ground, tipping her chin up to meet his gaze. She wasn't going to let him think anything about him intimidated her, and she certainly didn't want him thinking his nearness was turning her bones into a quivering mass of Jell-O. God, he smelled good. Like soap and leather and pine. She could see the smoldering desire in his eyes, and when he leaned forward, she nearly fell into his arms, ready for him to kiss her again.

"Cups?" He reached a hand to the cabinet behind her, brushing his other hand over her arm as he leaned past her.

Her heart leapt into her throat, racing, pounding hard enough that he had to be able to hear it. "Yeah," she answered dumbly, jumping away from his touch.

Smooth, Jennifer.

Clay poured himself a cup of coffee from the half-brewed pot and turned back to the couch, but not before she caught the smile slowly curving over his lips. He knew exactly how he affected her and was doing it deliberately, the jerk. She grabbed her own mug and slammed the cabinet, causing him to turn back to her.

"Problem?"

"Nothing a little coffee and some fresh air can't fix," she answered sweetly, pouring the cup and slipping on her boots.

"I'll feed. You sit. When I finish, I'll come back and help you make breakfast."

It was something they'd done together before his departure. When they were on the road, he'd help Mike or Scott feed the animals before joining her each morning while she made breakfast for the crew. Most of the time, in the cramped space of the fifth-wheel, they would bump into each other and end up pressed against the refrigerator, kissing and leaving breakfast behind entirely to make a quick detour to the bedroom. She dragged her wayward thoughts back to the present, forcing herself to remember that her detours had led to nothing but a broken heart and shattered promises. Clay had a way of distracting her that wasn't healthy for her state of mind.

"I don't need help, Clay. I've been—"

"I know, doing it yourself for the last five years," he finished for her. He looked up, pausing as he tugged on his boots, a frown curving his brow. "Jen, I know you don't *need* my help. You never have." He straightened his pant legs over the boots, stood, and walked over to her.

She took a step back, bumping against the counter as he reached out to brush his thumb over her cheek. "It was always that way with us, wasn't it? Maybe that was part of our problem."

He didn't give her a chance to respond as he headed out the door but not before she saw the sadness in his eyes, the regret, and wondered if he might not be right. Looking back, she'd tried to be everything to him—his coworker, his confidante, his friend, and his lover. It hadn't worked. She gave him every moment of every day, and he'd taken everything with him when he walked away. She raised her fingers to where his thumb had caressed her cheek, her skin still tingling with arousal. She wondered if she'd ever told him the truth.

"I *do* need you, Clay. I always have."

"Jennifer, come here." Mike didn't have to tell her he was disappointed in her. She could hear it loud and clear in his tone. "What is going on with you today?"

"I don't know."

She knew exactly what was going on. Her gaze slid over the cowboys on horseback who were waiting at the back gate of the arena for the next event to begin. Clay laughed with Scott, his hat pulled low on his forehead. His eyes met hers, and she looked away quickly. She had to get her head on straight. Having Clay at the rodeo was doing exactly what she had worried it would—distracting her, scattering her focus.

"You forgot the flag at the other end of the arena, you were late getting in before the calf roping, and now you lose your hat? Why don't you just let the queen do the flag runs? You can head up to the announcer's booth."

Tears of frustration burned behind her eyelids. "No, I'm fine," she insisted.

Mike followed the direction of her gaze as she looked toward Clay again. "No, you aren't." He laid a hand on her shoulder. "Go, take a break. Get some water or something. Have one of the boys take you to get your truck. Something."

"I'm fine," she repeated, hoping that saying it again would make it true.

"Jen, I hate to see you like this." Mike had never tried to be her father, even after he'd accepted guardianship of Jen and her brothers. But even though he'd been more like their cool uncle, she could see the parental concern in his eyes.

"Then don't hire him back, Mike. You know he's going to bail on you again."

Mike took a step backward. She could see her brutal honesty surprised him. "Jen, we need an experienced pickup man for Lancaster next weekend. I don't have time to find someone else, and we both know Derek isn't ready for something this serious."

"Please, Mike," she whispered, hating the weakness in her pleading. The longer Clay was around, the more danger to her heart.

"We don't have a choice unless we want to cancel next week's rodeo." They both knew they couldn't do that. Rodeo committees planned all year for these events, booking stock contractors at least twelve months in advance. "It's only one week," he promised.

Jen watched Mike walk away, hurrying back to the announcer's booth, and she wondered if he wasn't trying to escape. Without Silvie, their housekeeper and resident "mom" who had stayed behind to care for the ranch, Jen had no one who understood the emotional turmoil Clay caused in her. None of the men in her life were equipped to understand the confusing gamut of female emotions seeing him had woken. One minute she hated him, and the next she wanted to throw herself into his arms. She despised her weakness for wanting to be near him even as she loathed herself for pushing him away. How did you let go of the one person you wanted to hold onto the most?

She watched Clay working his event. He was majestic to watch on horseback. He looked like he was born to ride, moving with such fluidity that it could only be described as graceful, even if it wasn't a manly term. There was nothing feminine about him. Well over six feet of sheer muscle mass, he lifted bronc riders onto the backs of their horses like they were rag dolls. Yet, despite his size and brute strength, she knew from experience how gentle he could be. His touch had never been anything but tender, treating her like she was made of delicate porcelain. Except for the one part of her he chose to break.

She turned away from the gate and hurried to her trailer. She might as well start getting things packed up to head back to the ranch after the rodeo. Scott and Derek could stay and close up the deal with the rodeo committee. She was heading home tonight, even if it meant driving solo. She wasn't spending another night with Clay Graham on her couch if she could help it.

CLAY LOCKED THE door of the fifth-wheel as he came around from the front of the truck to where Mike was inspecting the back of the trailer. "Okay, the brake lights are fine. You're ready to go," Mike informed him.

"Whose bright idea was this again?" The broad smile that spread over Mike's face left no answer necessary. Clay rolled his eyes and shook his head. "Jen's made it pretty clear she doesn't want anything to do with me at this point."

Mike laughed at Clay. "You know Jen better than that by now. Give her a little time, and don't push." He grew serious for a moment. "She never stopped loving you, you know, but you really messed up when you left. You need to tell her why you did it. Don't you think you owe her at least that?"

Clay caught the keys Mike tossed his way in midair. "No. No way." He shook his head. "I'm not going to burden her with that."

"They're your family, Clay. A part of you. She's not going to see it as a burden. If you would have just been honest in the first place, you'd never been in this position now."

"I couldn't tell her then, and I'm not going to now, so let it go, Mike."

"If you don't tell her the truth, you'll never get her back," the older man warned.

"I didn't come here to get her back. I didn't even come here to get my old job back."

"Then why the hell *did* you come, Clay?" Mike took a step forward, standing toe-to-toe with him. Mike might think of Clay as family, but right now he was protecting the woman he'd raised as his daughter. "If you hurt her again..."

"I'm not trying to hurt her, Mike." Clay stepped back, letting the tension dissipate. He didn't want to fight with Mike, but he was right. His presence was hurting Jen. He either needed to fix this situation or walk away and never look back. "I'll make this right. I'll tell her as much as I can."

Mike shook his head in disbelief. "You can tell me or Scott, even Derek, but not her?"

"You guys won't try to fix the situation or fix me. You and Scott understand that this is something I had to deal with, that I'm *still* dealing with. You won't put yourselves into danger trying to help."

"And I thought I was clueless when it came to women," Mike muttered. "She's not trying to fix you; she's trying to share a life with you. That means the good and bad, in either of your lives. Including your past."

JEN STARED OUT the window, irritated that the macho chauvinist had insisted on driving. It was bad enough he was coming back to the ranch at all, but did he have to drive her truck too? She would much rather have driven home with Derek. Hell, she would have even driven one of the stock trailers if it would have kept her from sitting in the passenger seat next to Clay. And what in the world possessed Clay to let Derek drive his horses and rig back to the ranch tomorrow? The entire thing smelled like a setup, and she didn't like it.

"So, whose idea was it for you to drive back to the ranch with me and leave your rig with Derek?"

"They wouldn't tell me when I asked the same question." He glanced in her direction and grinned. "My money is on Mike."

"Or Scott," she suggested.

He pointed a finger at her in agreement. "You're probably right. Or they're in cahoots."

She arched her brow. "Cahoots? What are you, eighty? Who even says that?"

Maybe if they could talk about other things, other people, anything other than themselves and their past, this next week wouldn't be a disaster, and the rest of this three-hour drive home would be bearable. Maybe if they could find some common ground of friendship, they could avoid the land mines their past relationship seemed to trigger.

Clay gave her a lopsided smile. "I've missed this. We used to joke around all the time."

And there went any hope she held out for the next few hours. "Clay, don't," she warned.

"Don't what? You know, you never let me explain."

"Because you were kissing me, not explaining."

She saw his gaze shift in her direction, settling briefly on her mouth before he turned back to the road. "You didn't seem to mind."

"Don't mistake my apathy for enjoyment." She was lying through her teeth and they both knew it, but she wasn't about to confess anything to him.

"Apathy, huh?" He glanced her way again, and she shifted nervously under his heated gaze. "So, if I were to—"

"Don't go there. Find something else to talk about, or I'll turn the radio on and sing at the top of my lungs."

"Okay," he said with a chuckle. "Anything but that."

She knew he was kidding. It was common knowledge for anyone who'd spent time at the ranch that she loved country music, but she couldn't carry a tune in a bucket. She didn't care. She found pleasure in torturing those around her with her personal musical stylings, even if it was bad enough to send the barn cats into hiding.

This was the easy friendship she remembered between them, the relationship she regretted losing. She missed having him there to offer advice when Derek almost didn't graduate high school because a teacher accused him of losing a textbook. She missed laughing with him when Scott screamed like a woman after Derek dropped a rope by the water trough in the corral, making it look like a snake. She missed crying on his shoulder when she woke from another nightmare where her mother was reaching out from the fiery crash. More than anything else, she missed the way he would stand behind her and wrap his arms around her, making her feel completely enveloped and safe, while he whispered into her ear how far and wide and forever his love was.

Regret and longing twined in her chest, wrapping around her lungs and making her feel like she couldn't catch her breath. The playfulness of the moment was gone, lost again to her memories and the bitterness that always trailed closely behind. He seemed to sense the change in her and reached for the radio knob, in spite of his words.

"Wait." Her hand reached out and covered his. Electricity seemed to jump from the connection, traveling up her arm and shocking her heart. "Just tell me why you left. No excuses. One minute you were there and we were happy, and the next you were gone. Why?"

Clay withdrew his hand from under her fingers as if her touch burned. "Are you sure you want to do this here? Now?" His gaze met hers for a brief moment before returning to the road, but she could see the honesty in his eyes. And the fear. "I can't explain everything."

He ran a hand over his face. "The first thing you need to know is that I loved you from the first moment I saw you, Jennifer." When she didn't say anything, he went on. "I planned on marrying you, on spending the rest of my life with you, but after you said yes, I realized how little I had to offer you."

Clay shook his head. "I was only twenty-two, you were barely twenty, and you already had a family to take care of. I couldn't support all of you, and I didn't want to live off Mike's charity."

She interrupted him. "You think that's what we've done?"

"No, I…damn it. That's not what I meant." He looked at the road, avoiding her questioning gaze. "You three have built this company with Mike, but I'm just the loser who would have been milking my wife's hard work. I couldn't do that."

"Clay—"

"Hear me out. You deserved far more than I could ever offer you. I got scared you'd realize it, and I ran."

She could hear the anguish in his voice. "You left because you thought you weren't good enough for me? Clay, you never had to *earn* my love," she whispered. "It was always yours."

"I wanted to save you from making a mistake. And I had to close a few chapters of my life."

She stared at him, silent for so long that he finally turned to look at her. As much as she wanted to believe him, her instinct told her he was holding back. He said there were some things he couldn't explain. Couldn't or *wouldn't*, she wondered. This wasn't making sense.

"I was old enough to tell you I loved you, to share my bed with you, but not to make the decision to marry you?"

"I don't know how to explain what I was thinking. I thought you'd look back down the road and regret our life together, so I made the decision for you." He reached for the front of his baseball cap and shifted the hat on his head. "In retrospect, I made a mistake, but at the time, I thought I was doing the right thing. I was protecting you."

"I'm not buying this, Clay. I want to, believe me. What do you mean, 'protecting me'?"

He shifted his eyes back to the road, refusing to meet hers again. "I don't know what else you want me to say."

"The truth." She rubbed her hands along the top of her thighs, trying to work out the details in her mind. "Even if what you're telling me is true, why did you call Scott and Mike? Why didn't you ever return my calls? Why did you stay away so long?" She turned to face him, her hand at the back of the seat next to his shoulder. "Why did you come back now?"

The muscle in his jaw was ticking. She could see that wall rising up again, spreading the chasm between them and making her wonder if the gap was too wide to ever bridge.

"Clay, you wanted a chance to explain, so explain. I want to know, please."

He barely glanced her way, but she didn't miss the way his hands gripped the steering wheel, turning his knuckles white. Or the way his nostrils flared and his lips pinched together. Without saying another word, he reached forward and turned on the radio, effectively cutting off any further discussion and any hope she had for understanding what had gone wrong.

Chapter Five

JEN WOKE THE next morning to silence in the kitchen downstairs. Usually the cacophony of her brothers and Mike and any of the crew who snuck in to be fed by Silvie was enough to wake the dead. She glanced at her nightstand, wondering if she had overslept, but the clock simply blinked back at her, indicating that they'd lost power at some point after she'd fallen asleep last night. She flung the blankets back and jumped from the bed, hurrying to grab her cell phone from the dresser against the wall. If the sun filtering through her window was any indication, it was after eight, and she needed to get started grooming the horses before the boys arrived this afternoon.

She glanced at the phone. How in the world had she managed to sleep until nine? The horses must be starving by now. She rushed through her morning routine, only taking a quick swipe through her tresses with the brush before pulling her hair under a baseball cap and tossing on an old T-shirt with a comfortable pair of jeans. She slid her feet into her worn Ropers, hurrying down the stairs and into the kitchen.

"I already fed them." Clay sat at the kitchen table, sipping a cup of coffee, his legs crossed casually at the ankles.

"Uh, thanks?"

"Is that a question?" He quirked a brow as he took another sip of the brew. "I just started a fresh pot. Silvie headed into town to the grocery store before everyone comes home this afternoon." He pushed the chair in front of him out with his foot. "Sit, I'll fix you something for breakfast."

She wanted to sit, to pretend that this was what they did every day, like any normal couple. But they weren't a regular couple anymore. He'd turned his back on that normalcy. He'd even rejected her offer of forgiveness yesterday. If only he would explain. Then they could move forward, past this stubborn stalemate, into some semblance of tolerance.

Irritation at his blasé attitude burned in her chest as she moved toward the cabinet and reached for a travel mug, ignoring the chair. "I have work to do today. You know, horses to be ridden and groomed, and stalls to clean before the boys get home. But by all means, you should feel free to put your feet up and relax until they get home today." She grabbed a piece of fruit from the bowl Silvie kept filled on the kitchen table and clipped the lid over the top of her mug before waltzing out the back door.

She didn't have time to bicker with him today, but, oh, how the thought of the two of them, alone on the ranch, made an unwelcome sizzle of excitement spiral to parts of her long ignored.

CLAY WATCHED HER go, cursing himself for his stupidity. What the hell was wrong with him? He should have just told her the truth yesterday when she asked. His pride was going to ruin every good thing in his life, just like it always had. Jen would have understood the need to take care of family; she'd been doing it for years with her brothers. What she wouldn't understand was his need to leave again, to keep her safe from his past.

He walked to the back door and watched her head for the barn. Clay thought about following her for a second, but he'd never seen Jen like this before. Maybe Mike was right: he needed to be careful not to push her too much, but he wasn't about to let her get too far from his sight.

"I'll clean the stalls. Just go ahead and work the horses," he called after her. He saw her raise a hand in acknowledgment.

There was nothing friendly in her gesture, nothing to give him any hope that they might be able to rebuild their friendship. *At least she didn't flip me the bird.*

He wasn't sure why it even mattered, since he wasn't staying. Mike had asked him to stay for a week until Jake returned, so unless he wanted to marry the woman and put the whole family in jeopardy, he was just making it harder on both of them when it came time for him to leave.

Marry her? Where had that thought come from?

Jen had no intention of being in the same room as him right now, let alone marrying him. He'd had his chance, and he'd tossed it away.

Clay wandered onto the porch, watching Jen as she walked through the aisleway of the barn. Damn, that woman could stir him in ways no other could. She might be a tomboy, but beneath her rough-and-tumble exterior, she was all soft femininity. She'd always worked as hard as any of the men on the ranch, probably even harder. He remembered nights when she'd helped both Scott and Derek with their homework before heading back out to groom the animals after sending the boys off to bed. While they attended school, she'd worked her butt off on the ranch, sacrificing her own education to make sure they both got degrees. She hadn't taken the role of mothering them lightly. Nor had she slacked off on becoming a shrewd businesswoman. So far, she'd marketed their company better than any of them, helping the business grow from a small-town contractor to an elaborate, full-scale operation, with several full-time employees on the crew.

She was brilliant and beautiful. Clay continued to watch her from a distance, just like he'd done for nearly six months before she noticed him. Back then, he'd deliberately made himself invisible. He knew he didn't deserve someone like Jen. She was so far out of his league that he wasn't fit to clean her horse's stall. He'd been nothing more than a stall cleaner with a chip on his shoulder and a past he wanted to forget. A guy like him couldn't bring anything of value into her life. Some things hadn't changed with time.

Clay leaned over the porch railing, watching her saddle a big bay horse, a nice-looking gelding with two white socks and a blaze. He'd look great under saddle in the opening ceremonies, and Clay wondered if that was what she had planned for him.

Jen had a good life with Mike and her brothers. It wasn't right to drag her down with the problems that plagued his family. It was part of why he'd left. He'd wanted to protect her from the trouble that seemed to follow him like a karmic gift from hell. The last few text messages he'd received from his sister weren't making him feel too optimistic that his life was on an upswing now either. No, if he really cared about Jen, he'd make himself invisible for the next week and then vanish from her life again.

Jen stumbled, falling against the horse's rump and glanced back in his direction. She knew he was watching her and was trying not to catch his eye, but it didn't deter him in the slightest. For the past five years, he'd had to make due with only a picture and his memories. He wasn't about to shortchange himself when he had the flesh-and-blood woman in front of him. He'd forgotten little things about her that he'd loved: the way she walked, with her chin just slightly dipped down and her shoulders back as if daring the world to test her; her eyes that dared defiance but, at the same time, showed a compassion he'd rarely seen from anyone else; the way her hips swayed just slightly, rolling with a feminine grace that came from feeling comfortable in her own athletic skin rather than practiced flirtation. She was all woman, and at one time, she'd been all his.

He spun on his heel and walked back into the house, unable to bear the jealousy twisting his gut. Just because he'd been her first, didn't mean he was her last. Who knew how many men she'd dated since he left? He deliberately hadn't asked Scott about her love life. He hadn't wanted to know, but now he was curious why she was still single when she didn't have to be. She mustn't be dating anyone now. She'd have told him, if for no other reason than to remind him of what he'd lost, and he wondered why she was still alone. He knew Jen always planned on having a family of her own, outside of raising her brothers. Now that they were grown men, or well on their way, why was she still devoting all of her time to her brothers and the company? A twinge of hope rose. Could it be that she still had feelings for him?

The soft *clomp* of shod hooves on the dirt caught his attention, and he hurried to the front door in time to see her head out across the pasture toward the lake. She pulled her hat low on her brow, but he didn't need to see her face to know she was upset. He could speculate why. It didn't take a brain surgeon to figure out his presence back at the ranch had her pissed off and ready to do battle.

He left the house, crossed the yard, and ran into the barn, where he retrieved a bridle from the tack room, slipping it over the halter on a sorrel mare. Jumping on her bareback, he followed Jen, hanging back far enough that she wouldn't notice him. He watched her ride, letting the horse open up to a full gallop. The lake had always been her refuge when she felt circumstances closing in on her. Clay hated himself for causing the turmoil within her. He shouldn't have gone to the rodeo, he shouldn't have let Mike talk him into coming back here, and he never should have kissed Jen.

Clay debated turning back to the barn, waiting for Derek to show up with his trailer so he could head out instead of staying. He should get his ass back to Oregon and let Jen move on with the life she'd made without him. Wasn't that what he was planning on doing next week anyway?

"Not now." The words came out on a breath without him realizing he was even speaking them. But once they were out, Clay knew it was the absolute truth. He didn't want to go back to Oregon.

The truth was that his past had caught up to him almost five years ago when his brother had overdosed. Then his mother died two years later. Now, it was only his sister, Candie, who needed his help. Trouble seemed to follow her like a stray dog after scraps. And, if he was honest with himself, he was tired of being the one-man cleanup crew for his family. If he wanted to stay—and God help him, he did—he simply needed to tell Jen the truth about his past and let her make the decision.

"But you won't, because there's always that chance something might come up," he muttered to himself. He would never allow anything to hurt Jen.

If that were true, then why was he still here?

JENNIFER COULD TIE the gelding near the trees and let him graze without worrying about him spooking, but she knew how much Gunner liked to play in the water. She held the lead rope loosely in her fingers, allowing the colt to wade into the edge of the lake, almost to his knees. She smiled as he pawed at the water, splashing it over his belly and chest, flipping his nose up and down. Droplets hit her where she sat on a log near the shore. She laughed at the gelding's antics but stopped suddenly when chills ran down her spine.

She looked over her shoulder, scanning the horizon, unsure of what she was even searching for. Gunner wandered closer to her, rubbing his rough upper lip at her thigh, and she turned her attention back to him, reaching up to pat his shoulder. He was a good horse, and she was looking forward to using him at the next few rodeos. His head shot up, and he looked behind them, snorting loudly with alarm.

"What is it, buddy?" She stood up, turning to see what had riled him. She could barely make out a horse and rider cresting the hill, but she'd recognize Clay's massive physique anywhere. "I should've known."

She watched as he rode toward her and wondered if it would be easier to mount up and head back to the barn or let him come and simply ignore his presence. What difference would it really make? He obviously had no interest in sharing why he'd left, and she wasn't willing to forgive him until he was honest with her. Maybe he'd get bored if she ignored him and leave her alone. Wasn't that what he did best?

The warmth that circled south of her belt buckle surprised her. No, there were other things he did far better. Jennifer stared at Clay's hands as he slid them over the mare's neck, dismounting and walking her toward the tree line. Jen couldn't help but remember the way those hands...She yanked the reins on her wandering imagination and walked Gunner back to the trees as well, looping his rope over a low branch with enough length for him to graze on the spring grass. She went back to the edge of the water, returning to her log, and picked up a handful of pebbles, toying with them as Clay approached.

The way he acted like he belonged here irritated her, as if he hadn't been gone for the last five years. But at one time he did belong, knew the property as well as she and her brothers did, maybe even better. Now, it just felt like he was a traitor.

"You okay?" he asked. She glanced back at him as he tied his mare near Gunner and headed toward her, stopping before he reached her, as if she were a flight risk and he didn't want to get close enough to frighten her.

She wasn't the one who had run away.

"Fine, why?" The nonchalance she'd been trying for wasn't what she heard in the sharp note of her voice.

Clay shrugged and sat down on the other end of the log. It wasn't wide, but it felt like miles separated them instead of less than a foot. "You only come here when you're upset." He gave her a sideways glance, a grin pulling at the corner of his mouth. "Unlike your brothers."

She knew he was trying to break the tension between them, but it was hard for her to just turn off the storm brewing inside. She shook her head and looked across the lake, avoiding the deep emerald of his eyes.

"What did they call it?" He chuckled.

"Make-Out Lake."

"They always did have a way with the ladies." Clay rolled his eyes and shook his head. "Who named it that anyway?"

"Knowing those two, your guess is as good as mine. Could have been either one." She felt a smile tugging at the corners of her lips. Why was it so easy to fall back into companionable conversation with him? Why couldn't she stay angry and bitter? She watched him search the ground and wondered what he was doing until he got up and picked up a flat rock, jostling it in his hand.

"You'd better not start anything you can't finish."

Clay turned to face her, his eyes growing hot and dark, and she felt the heat rise to her cheeks as she realized how he could misconstrue her comment. She tried to recover quickly. "You know I can skip a rock three times as far as you can."

"How do you know I haven't been practicing?" he asked, playfully challenging her, a dimple creasing his cheek.

Jen arched a brow. *Challenge accepted.*

He knew her well enough to know that she would never let him make a claim he couldn't back up. "Let's see what you've got, big shot." She dropped the pebbles from her hand and rose from the log, searching the bank for a few perfect skipping rocks.

Clay laughed, flicking his wrist and casting a rock over the water's surface. One...two...three...four. On his first one? His smile widened and his eyes filled with laughter. Jen's heart thudded almost painfully in her chest and her breath caught. Man, she'd really missed that smile. Did he have any clue how sexy he really was?

She bit her lip. "Do I have to go three times the distance or just farther?"

"We probably should have laid the ground rules before I threw. Let's say the winner is whoever gets the most skips." He reached for another rock from the ground, bouncing it in his hand, checking the shape and weight like a pro.

She eyed him with distrust. "What's the prize?"

"What do you want?" His voice was husky, laced with innuendo, and she felt his gaze as it traveled over her.

Every limb in her body went weak as heat coursed through her, pooling in places only he seemed to awaken. Her chest heaved as she tried to catch her breath, the heat of his gaze drawing her closer to him, making her want to run her hands over him, to feel the valleys of hard muscle while his lips and hands banished their history in the wake of desire.

Realization dawned. As much as she wanted to believe it was just lust she felt for Clay, it wasn't true. She still loved him and needed him as much as she ever had. It didn't matter how badly he'd hurt her. She *wanted* to forgive him, still wanted to be his wife, and that insight was too dangerous to ever admit out loud.

"If I win, you leave and never come back."

It physically hurt to say the words, but she tried to hide it by bending over, pretending to search for the perfect stone. In reality, she was trying to still the agony twisting and curling in her chest, squeezing her lungs and burning in the back of her eyes. She blinked back tears. She couldn't look at him, couldn't see that her wager meant nothing to him either way.

Clay took a long inhale and picked up two more stones as he considered her terms. "Best of three wins." He dug a stone from the soft dirt on the bank. "But if I win, you have to have dinner with me."

Her gaze snapped up to meet his. She stood, her shoulders ramrod stiff, before taking a step backward. "Dinner? That's it?" She looked at him with skepticism.

He shrugged. "Okay, dinner and you give me a kiss."

Under normal circumstances, this bet would be a no-brainer. She'd been skipping rocks since she could walk and won every time her brothers challenged her. But she'd just seen what he did on a cold throw. It might be dumb luck, but Clay wasn't the type to make a bet on a whim. He was cautious, calculating. It also made her wonder why he chose something as simple as a kiss for his reward. By the look in his eyes, he was teasing her. She was nothing more than a game to him. A way to pass the time. She was a fool to think he might care. Win or lose, neither bet mattered to him in the end. He was still leaving at the end of the week.

She thrust out her hand defiantly. "Deal."

His gaze fell to her mouth, and he gave her a cocky grin, ignoring her still extended hand. "Your throw."

Jennifer bounced the flat stone in her hand, turned sideways and cocked her arm back. With a flick of her wrist, she sent the stone sailing, skimming the surface of the water.

"Ha! Five!" She did a little victory dance on the spot.

Clay chuckled at her antics. "Don't celebrate just yet." He tossed his stone, matching hers skip for skip. "That was five. Now what?"

She repeated her movements, garnering only four this time, tying up their score. Clay smiled down at her. "Do you want to go, or do you want to have the last to throw?"

"Go right ahead." She didn't want to admit she was nervous. He *must* have been practicing. There was a very real chance she might lose this bet. "I wouldn't want you to claim it wasn't a fair match."

Even if the thought of being kissed by him again made her feel like molten lava inside, she wasn't going to let him see it.

"Trust me, it wasn't." Clay let his last stone fly, and she watched in shock as it skipped five, six, *seven times*. On her best day, with a perfect stone, she had never made one skip that many times. Dread curled in her belly, winding around her lungs and gripping her heart. How was she going to be in his arms and *not* react to his touch, to not let him see how he was affecting her?

"Are you going to throw, or do you want to admit defeat now?" He winked at her, the dimple creasing his cheek again.

"I'm not admitting anything." She bristled and her senses were on high alert, knowing her fate was as good as sealed.

Clay laughed. "Okay, then throw already." Jennifer glared at him and tossed her stone, watching as it sank after only three skips. "That was pathetic. You want one more try?"

"And let you say I cheated? No way." She planted her fists on her hips. Irritation flared in her chest at being bested. "Let's get this over with."

She knew she was being abrasive to hide the emotions bubbling to the surface like a geyser, ready to erupt. The way he ignored her, sitting back down on the log, made her wonder if he didn't know it as well. She'd had a chance to remove the cause of her anxiety, not to mention the ache in her heart, and she'd blown it. Unfortunately, only her head was disappointed. Her body, betraying her, broke out with goose bumps at the thought of his touch.

"In a minute. Come, sit."

He was up to something, and the suspicion sent a shiver of anticipation through her.

CLAY WAS STALLING, and it was driving her crazy. Jennifer didn't like losing at anything. As far as she was concerned, it meant she wasn't as in control as she wanted to believe, and Jen had to feel in control of everything. He wasn't going to let her rush this. He wanted to savor the moment leading up to kissing her, to enjoy the buildup of yearning and need he could feel throbbing in his veins. He could see the quick pulse in her neck as she sat; she was trying to ignore him and failing miserably. He watched her bite her lip and almost groaned at the tiny gesture, wishing it were his teeth biting her, his tongue soothing the flesh.

Longing raced through his blood, centering in his core, as he focused on every detail of her. She tucked a stray hair, blowing in the breeze, behind her ear before glancing his way, as if he wouldn't notice her watching him. He almost laughed as she wiped her palms over her thighs, slapping them against her legs.

"Okay, I'm sitting. Now what?"

"You never told me what's bothering you enough to bring you to Make-Out Lake."

"I told you, nothing. I'm fine."

He narrowed his eyes and edged closer to her on the log. "I don't believe you."

"Believe what you want." She rose. "Either take your kiss now or I'm leaving."

He raised his brows at her false bravado. He could see her flush at the mention of kissing him. It was killing him to wait, to tease her with the anticipation, but he wanted her to admit, if only to herself, how much she wanted him before he took another step toward repairing their broken relationship. He might be a fool for even trying, but he wanted her forgiveness as much as he wanted her heart.

"In that big of a hurry to kiss me?"

She rolled her eyes. "It will be a cold day in hell before I kiss you."

Clay lips curved upward. "Ah, but that was the bet. You kiss me. Not the other way around." He saw her pale as she realized he was right; he'd chosen the words for the bet deliberately. He knew she'd been suspicious, but she obviously hadn't expected this.

Standing up, he took a step toward her. "You sure you wouldn't rather talk a little bit more, maybe tell me what was bothering you earlier? You know, keep stalling?"

She clenched her jaw, her eyes darkening, and he knew he'd hit the bull's-eye. He wasn't certain whether the look in her eyes was desire or anger, but he felt the sizzle down his back at the thought of finding out. It didn't take much to imagine how right it felt to kiss her, how she could make his blood boil with need, make him want to lock them both in a room and throw away the key. As long as he was with her, the rest of the world could be damned.

"Fine." She walked up to him, pulling her hat from her head, her hips swaying slightly in the feminine way she had about her and stood on tiptoe to press a kiss to his cheek, bracing herself with a hand on his shoulder. "There, debt paid until dinner."

He inhaled the sweet scent of her, like honey and sunshine in early summer. He reached for her hand, his fingers winding around her wrist. "That wasn't a kiss and you know it."

His gaze bore into hers, making sure she knew exactly what he was doing. His arm wound around her waist, pulling her against him, her curves molding against every hard plane of him. He ducked his head toward her, stealing her breath, his lips finding hers. He meant to tease her, to remind her of what they'd shared—what they could again—but as soon as his mouth met hers, his self-control disappeared. His hand slid up her spine, his fingers curling against the back of her head as his tongue sought hers, branding her. Her hands, braced between them only moments before, gripped at his shoulders, silently pleading for more.

Clay's body answered her yearning with his own, the torment driving him mad. He wanted her, here and now, on the grass at the edge of the water, in the lake. Hell, he'd lie on the rocks as long as it meant she would continue touching him. His entire body was aflame, as if the spark of desire he'd carried for her the last five years had exploded into an inferno, consuming him. His hands couldn't stop moving, wanting to touch every inch of her, from her velvety smooth cheek to the satiny skin of her waist under her shirt, where his thumbs ran along the edge of her bra. His mouth moved to the hollow of her neck, dipping to taste the arching column of her throat as her head fell back into his hand. His entire body throbbed with need, aching to be surrounded by her.

Her hands slipped under the sides of his shirt, her fingertips trailing over his ribs, tickling him even as it made him groan with longing. She tugged at the material, and he jerked it off, following with her shirt, throwing them to the side. Jennifer's fingers dug into the muscles of his back, pressing her breasts against him. He could feel her nipples, hard even through her bra, against his chest. Clay wanted to stop and take time to look at her, to see the curves that hadn't been there before, but he was too afraid she would remember who he was, what he'd done, and leave him standing here, alone and broken. He needed her and right now. With her in his arms, he couldn't remember why he'd ever thought leaving her was a good idea. Nothing had ever satisfied him the way loving her had. It was a mistake to have left her when she offered him every part of her—body and soul.

His hands cupped her rear, lifting her against him, allowing her to feel all of him, straining at the confining material of his pants. Her hands slid around his neck, drawing him back to her sweet mouth. Her tongue swept against his, dancing, toying, teasing the desire already raging out of control. His fingers twisted the clasp of her bra, slid the straps down her arms, and tossed the wisp of material near her shirt. His hand moved to cup her, testing the weight as he brushed his thumb over the peak, and she cried out. He had to see her, to taste her. Clay bent his head, kissing the valley between her breasts as her fingers curled into his hair.

Dear God, this woman could drive him mad. He flicked the bud, circling it, before taking it into his mouth, suckling her flesh. Jen gripped his shoulders as he wrapped one arm behind her, pulling her closer. Her whimper of need broke through the haze of his adoration. She was beautiful, her body rounded curves of sculpted perfection. He unbuckled her belt and slid her jeans down her thighs.

This is a mistake.

The thought reverberated through his mind. She'd asked him to leave, made that her prize if she'd won. If he let this go further, she would hate him even more than she already did. She might want him, but he'd killed any love she felt. He wanted her forgiveness, not regret. He wanted her to look at him the way she used to, like he was her hero, instead of with the disappointment he'd seen in her eyes at the rodeo. He fell to his knees and dropped his forehead against her stomach, forcing himself to keep his eyes closed, even as she tried to catch her breath. It was killing him with the most exquisite kind of torture. He sucked in a ragged breath and kissed the curve of her abdomen. His erection strained against his jeans painfully.

"Don't stop."

He couldn't have possibly heard her whispered plea correctly. Indecision ripped at him.

"Clay, please." Her palms moved over his face to cup his jaw. "Please."

He was lost. After the way he'd hurt her, the agony he heard in her voice was his undoing. He would give them this, this one last memory of a love they once shared.

"Jen." Her name was a prayer on his lips as they moved against her stomach, his breath fanning over the delicate flesh. His hand slid over her inner thigh, his thumb brushing against the moist center of her desire as she bit back a cry, her body bucking against him.

Clay rose and removed his pants, kicking them aside, and cupped her face in his hands. "Are you sure?"

"No," she answered honestly, her dark eyes glimmering with what he hoped weren't tears.

"Jen—"

"Clay, just shut up and love me like you used to."

Clay knew he would hate himself later, but right now, with her hands reaching for him, he couldn't deny either of them. He walked her toward the long, spring grass and lay on the ground, letting his body cradle hers. Jen pressed kisses over his chest before her mouth found his again. He let her take the lead, ready to let her go if she asked him to, all the while praying she wouldn't. She straddled him, and Clay lifted her hips, guiding her over him slowly, growling at the long-awaited ecstasy. His thumb found the center of her pleasure, stroking her until her neck arched, her long hair trailing down her back to tickle the tops of his thighs.

Jen gave herself over to the primal need, riding him; her fingers gripped his ribs as he plunged into her, his hands cupping her breasts. He wanted to stop time and hold this moment forever. Her body clutched him, making control impossible, and he curved one hand through her hair, dragging her down to him so that he could be completely surrounded by her, every part of them connected as he watched her climax wash over her.

Guilt swept through him as he tasted her hot tears mingled with the passion of their kiss. She collapsed against his chest, her breathing as ragged as his own as he struggled to reconcile what he'd allowed to happen. It was supposed to be a kiss, a reminder. He'd wanted her to crave his presence again, not drive her to regret his return. He wasn't even sure what to say.

"Jen?" He brushed a lock of hair behind her ear and pressed a kiss to her forehead before skimming his fingers over her back. She tensed under his hands.

"Oh, God," she whispered.

Her face was buried against his neck, but he could feel her emotional retreat. "No, don't. Don't move," he begged.

His hands moved around her, encircling her, pulling her as close as he could against him. "Please." He whispered the word into her hair.

"Stay away, Clay." He could hear the anguish in her voice, the self-loathing. "I can't do this again."

"Jen…"

"No!" Now he heard the panic creeping in as she moved away from him, plucked her clothes from the ground, and threw them on quickly. "Don't," she ordered, holding up a hand as he rose and pulled his pants on.

He could see her tears, leaving twin trails of pain on her face, as she ran to her horse. She quickly tightened the cinch and put the bridle over the horse's head. She galloped back toward the house as the tears coursed down her cheeks. He barely heard her pained whisper as she rode past, leaving him standing at the bank.

"Wasn't supposed to happen."

No, he silently agreed, *it wasn't.* But he realized now, she was as vital to him as his heartbeat, and his need for her was just as impossible to control. If he wanted any hope of a future with her, he had to make her forgive him, make her see how impossible it was for them to be apart any longer.

Chapter Six

CLAY SAT ON the front porch, staring down at the diamond solitaire glinting between his finger and thumb as the dying sunlight caught its faceted surface. He'd never wanted it back. In fact, he'd spent the last five years avoiding rodeos where he might see Jen and find that not only had she never forgiven him, but she'd also moved on. After what happened between them that morning, he knew what he really wanted was to put the ring back on her finger. To find a way back to the path they'd once been on. And there was only one way to do that.

He was a fool to even consider staying, and the cryptic text message his sister had sent him this afternoon didn't make him feel any more confident about his decision. Maybe if he could just break through his stubborn pride and explain to Jen why he'd left, *what* he'd been trying to protect her from, she might be willing to give him another chance. If their rendezvous at the lake didn't

84 T. J. KLINE

prove the fire between them still burned out of control, he didn't know what would. But he had to make sure his past wasn't going to come back to put her in any kind of danger. He had to know it was behind him, with no chance of ruining his future.

"How'd you end up with that again?"

Clay looked over at Scott, leaning against the doorway. He'd been so lost in his thoughts, he hadn't even heard Scott come out. "Jen gave it back after I found her in the bar." He slid the solitaire over the tip of his finger.

"Really?" Scott looked surprised as he flopped into one of the wicker chairs on the porch. "She's had it with her the whole time?"

"I guess." Clay wasn't sure what Scott was getting at.

"Maybe my sister hasn't quite given up on you."

Clay scowled. "Then why am I holding it?" He didn't need Scott reminding him how he'd screwed up, or what he'd lost. He was perfectly capable of throwing a one-man pity party; he didn't need Scott's help.

"Because you didn't listen. You pushed her buttons and she pushed back."

"I saved her butt from being mauled by bikers in a bar. Then drove her home. That's not pushing."

"Have you met my sister? When did she ever ask you to be her Prince Charming and rescue her? She doesn't need your protection. She never has." Scott shook his head. "Besides, I know you, Clay. You probably had her cornered out here last night, trying to apologize again."

"You'd be wrong." Clay looked back at the ring. The memory of her hands on him at the lake, the way she cried out his name as she found release, held enough power to send his blood coursing through his veins, settling in places he'd rather it didn't. He wasn't about to tell Scott how he'd molested Jen at the lake.

Scott shrugged. "Whatever you did, I'll bet you didn't tell her the truth about why you left, did you?" He rose and leaned toward Clay. "Look, if you want her back, and from your pitiful puppy dog eyes, I think you do, then you're going to have to open up and be honest with her. Until you do that, you've got a snowball's chance in hell."

Scott trotted down the stairs and across the front yard toward the barn, not even giving Clay the chance to make a retort. He wasn't sure where Scott got off giving any sort of advice when his own ex-fiancée had cheated on him with his best friend. He wasn't exactly a relationship expert.

But even he knew Scott was right. Jen had always been able to see right through him. She knew he wasn't being honest, and until he was, he might as well head right back up to Oregon because nothing short of honesty would be enough for her.

JEN GRIMACED AS she sipped at the coffee in her mug that had gone cold long ago. She rubbed her hand over her eyes, wishing dreams about Clay hadn't kept her tossing and turning all night or from focusing this morning. As she left the barn, heading to the house to refill her cup, a beat-up sedan limped down the driveway and pulled to a stop in front of the house. Silvie poked her head out the kitchen door on the side of the house, but

Jen waved her off, letting her know she'd greet the visitor.
A young woman unfolded herself from the driver's seat
and looked around, whistling low under her breath. By
the sweat-stained tank top and disheveled sandy blond
hair, Jen guessed she been driving hard and fast. As if
confirming her assumption, the Toyota belched exhaust
and seemed to sigh in relief as the woman reached back
in and turned it off.

"Can I help you?" Jen asked.

"Nice place, if horses are your thing." She shot Jen
a smile meant to disarm, but Jen only raised a brow in
question. The woman wasn't put off that easily. "I'm looking for someone and was told I could find him here." Jen
continued to look at the woman, letting her fill in the
silence. "Clay Graham?"

"Clay won't be back to the house until later." Relief
flooded the woman's face, and Jen wondered about her
connection to him. She'd never seen the woman before,
but there was something about her that looked familiar,
Jen just couldn't put her finger on what it was.

"Awesome." The woman slammed the car door, and
Jen was surprised it didn't break off. The woman bounced
onto the front porch and threw herself onto the wicker
love seat as if she owned the place without another glance
Jen's direction.

Jen's brows arched in surprise at the woman's audacity.
She pulled her cell phone from her pocket, dialing Scott's
number. "Who should I say is waiting?" *Since I assume
your butt planted on my porch means you're staying.*

"Just tell him Candie is looking for him."

And I'll just bet it's with an i, Jen thought, trying to ignore the jealousy curling in chest.

She heard Scott pick up the phone. "Hey, can you let Clay know he has a visitor here? Candie." She heard the cursing in the background and what sounded like fighting for the phone.

"Jen, tell her I'll be right there and then get everyone into the house and stay put."

"Excuse me?" She eyed the woman with her feet planted on the wicker table, watching as Silvie poked her head out and asked if Candie would like a drink. "Don't tell me we can't be hospitable."

"Jen, I mean it. You and Silvie get in the house and stay there until I get back. Is there anyone else with her?"

"No," she whispered, moving so their visitor couldn't hear her side of the conversation. "She's alone. Clay, what is this about?"

"Just promise me you'll go inside." She heard the truck doors slam shut and the sound of Scott's truck firing up. "We'll be there in just a couple of minutes."

Without waiting for her reply, Clay hung up, piquing her curiosity. Who was Candie, and why didn't he want Jen to talk to her? He certainly hadn't sounded thrilled at her arrival, which made Jen even more curious about the woman. She made her way to the porch. "He should be back in a few minutes. Are you hungry?" She barely got the words out before Silvie came out with iced tea and a plate of chocolate chip cookies.

"Wow, you both know how to make a person feel welcome."

She focused her hazel eyes on each of them in turn, almost as though assessing whether they were friends or foes. Jen could see wariness in the depths of her eyes, even if she was trying to hide it. Candie reached for one of the cookies tentatively, as if waiting for someone to slap her hand. Her words might be friendly but her actions were cautious.

"Where are you from, honey, if you don't mind my asking?" Silvie asked. "You look like you've been driving for quite a ways."

The woman sighed and dropped her head against the back of the couch, her blond hair billowing out like a curtain. "I was in New Mexico for a while, and then I headed to Idaho and spent some time there. I've been trying to get a hold of Clay, and when I was in Oregon I thought we could catch up for old times' sake, but they told me that he was here for a while." She jerked her chin at the car, sagging on the driveway. "I don't know how much farther that piece of junk will take me."

Jen watched the woman, curious about her relationship to Clay. He'd never mentioned a Candie, but then again, he'd never really talked about anything before or after his time on the ranch.

The woman was about the same age as Jen, maybe a bit younger, but she seemed calloused, as if life had dealt her far more of her share of hard times and less rainbows and sunshine than young women dreamed of. She was pretty, with a light dusting of freckles over her tanned cheeks and her hair pulled back from her face by a pair of cheap dollar-store sunglasses, but Jen didn't miss the worn tank top, ratty jeans, or the smell of several-day-old sweat. She knew Clay wouldn't warn her for nothing, but she couldn't help but feel sympathetic toward the exhausted woman.

"Candie, it will still be a little while before Clay gets here. Did you want to freshen up? Maybe take a shower?"

"What?" Candie's brows pinched together.

What was she thinking? For all she knew, this woman could be Clay's girlfriend. *Or wife.* Jen didn't want to be caught in the middle of whatever conversation Candie had planned for Clay. She should send her to the diner in town and tell Clay to meet her there. But another look at the fatigue lining Candie's eyes made Jen rethink her options. She would probably regret it, but this woman needed a warm shower and some food in her belly.

"Why don't you go take a shower, we'll throw your clothes in the wash, and you can relax for a bit. Silvie will show you where to go." Jen rose and headed down the steps. "I'll let Clay know you're inside when he gets here."

So FAR, CLAY had been able to stave off Jen and Scott's questions about Candie. He couldn't believe Jen had ignored everything he said and let Candie commandeer one of the guest rooms in the house. Jen usually read people far better. Why, in all that was holy, would she have fallen for Candie's sweet-girl act? He tossed the clean, folded clothes on the end of the bed where Candie was snoring lightly under a thin blanket. He wanted to scold himself for immediately glancing at the insides of her arms before he kicked the leg of the bed, but it wasn't like he didn't have a reason to check.

"Wake up, time to leave." He heard the callousness in his voice and sighed, hating this side of himself. But he wasn't going to have Jen, or anyone else, in danger because of him and his family.

Candie sat up in her borrowed clothes and rubbed her eyes. "No need to be rude, Clay. If you'd have answered my messages, I wouldn't have had to drive all the way to California trying to chase you down."

"What do you want?" He glanced over his shoulder, making sure the bedroom door was shut. "Better yet, were you followed this time?"

She pursed her pouty lips and rolled her eyes. "Well, it's good to see you again, too, big brother." She flipped her legs over the side of the bed and stood up, making her way to the window, pulling back the curtain and looking outside. "This is a nice place. No wonder you stayed here so long before." She looked back at him, still standing by the bed. "That woman downstairs is pretty. Is that the one you told me about?"

Clay sighed again, refusing to answer his sister. "How much do you need this time?" She shrugged a too-slim shoulder, and he wondered how much she'd actually been eating. "Candie, are you on the run again?"

"No." She answered too quickly and wouldn't meet his eye. It was a sure sign she was in trouble. "I mean, I owe a few people a little money, and I did stiff the guy who supposedly fixed my car but—"

"Damn it!" Clay spun around and ran a hand through his hair. His sister didn't ever owe a *little* money to anyone. She was a con artist, and one of these days it was going to get her killed. "Who, how much, and what for this time? Do they know where you are?"

"Apparently, this guy is claiming that I owe him nearly two Gs for some stuff I sold for him. I know I gave it all to him, but he's not exactly the reasonable type, if you know what I mean."

"Drugs?"

"No." She let the curtain drop and faced him, not bothering to elaborate on her answer. "Then there's the guy in Idaho from the bar. He didn't like a girl beating him at pool."

"You mean hustling him?"

She shrugged again. "Tomato, tomahto. So, are you going to loan me the money?"

"Why, so you can get high again or blow it gambling?"

She threw her shoulders back and stomped toward him, stabbing her finger at his chest. "For your information, I've been clean for two years." Clay arched a brow in disbelief. "After we found Bobby, I went off the deep end, but when Mom died…" She shook her head as if clearing away the painful memories. "I haven't touched anything since. After what happened to Bobby, I just…"

Her words trailed off. Clay knew Candie didn't like to talk about their brother. His *half*-brother. His mother had never realized the difference between love and lust and, as a result, often found herself on the disappointing end of the latter. When she'd finally learned her lesson, three kids later, she'd been forced to eke out a living in a dumpy apartment at the edge of a foothill town known for its rough crowd.

Still, she'd encouraged Clay to get as far away as possible, leaving behind the shady things he'd done as a teen to make ends meet for them. She'd claimed it was one less mouth to try to feed, but he knew better. She saw his desire to escape and loved him enough to push him to take it. At least until they'd found Bobby in a ditch from what appeared to be an overdose. That's when she gave in and called him, begging him to come back. Clay promised his mother he wouldn't let his youngest sister follow the same path.

However, old habits were hard to break, and so far, trying to help Candie was proving to be a slow Two-Step with danger. After their mother had finally lost her struggle with cancer, he had checked Candie into a rehab facility, making sure she was settled in before taking a job with Smith Brothers. It was the only thing he could do that would pay the bills for her treatment. He sent the money directly to the facility, making a conscious effort to stay in contact with Candie without connecting himself to the trouble that seemed to dog her steps. He looked at his sister. Candie had been clean, sober, and out of rehab for nearly two years. Until last week, she'd kept herself mostly out of harm's way, only hustling once in a while to make up the difference when waitressing tips slowed down. It had been a long time since Candie had caused any trouble or needed anything from him, and it had been nearly six months since he'd heard from her. Deep down, he'd hoped things were on an upswing. Otherwise, he'd never have agreed to haze for his buddies at the rodeo. He'd suspected there was a good chance he'd run into Jen. But, even knowing that she most likely hated him, the thought of *not* seeing her was just too much, so he'd taken the chance.

Now, just as he was trying to pave the way for a reconciliation with Jen, Candie's troubles were going to ruin any chance he had. Not to mention, get someone hurt.

"You need to go. I'll give you some money to pay these guys off, and you'd better pay them, but you need to leave." He grasped her elbow roughly, moving her toward the door.

"What's the big rush? Jennifer said I could stay for dinner."

"You are *not* staying and putting her in danger, Candie. She doesn't know about you or our past, and she's not going to."

JENNIFER HEARD FOOTSTEPS in the barn as she set the saddle onto the metal rack. Scott and Derek were in the house cleaning up before dinner, and she doubted Mike would be out here. She inhaled deeply through her nose, the dust making her want to sneeze.

Please don't let it be Clay. I can't do this right now.

She'd made sure she was scarce when he arrived at the house but knew Silvie had alerted him to Candie's presence. The woman upstairs had barely made it to the bed before she collapsed from exhaustion. Silvie wanted to feed her, but the bed had taken priority. Jennifer hadn't wanted to disturb her, so she'd headed outside to finish chores. She hadn't thought Clay would come out here when there was a woman just inside the house who had driven days searching for him.

She came out of the tack room with a bucket of brushes in one hand and fly spray in the other. She couldn't help the shiver of anticipation that traveled up her spine and settled over her shoulders like a warm sweater when Clay turned his gaze on her.

"I was hoping to find you out here."

Jennifer stared at him, silently, not sure whether she wanted to move toward him or run away. It didn't really matter, since she couldn't seem to get her feet moving anyway. His eyes seemed to glow from within, but she didn't want to name the emotion she could easily read on his face. Her brain finally connected the synapses to get her legs to react, and she took a step backward.

Where are you going?

She didn't know and she didn't care. Right now, all she wanted was to not be caught by the longing in his eyes that warned her he was about to kiss her again.

"Jen, don't. Don't run away from me." She heard the pleading note in his voice, but instead of feeling sympathetic, something in her snapped.

"I'm not the one who runs, Clay. That's you."

She was grateful for the horse tied in the aisle and ducked behind the mare, putting more distance between them. She set the bucket on the ground and reached for a curry comb, rubbing the animal down. "I don't have anything to run from. You're the one with one woman waiting in the house for you while you chase me down in the barn." She hoped he could see the fury in her eyes, the pent-up anger at his betrayal that was flooding her body.

He moved around the back of the horse, as quick as a rattlesnake strike, and grabbed her hand, turning her to face him. "I left because I had to. I wasn't running."

"Bullshit!"

She didn't want to hear his excuses or his lies. The venom that had been festering in her for the last five years poured into her blood, seeping from the wound that had never healed in her heart. She threw the comb into the bucket and shoved him away from her. The movement did little to give her the space she needed to move away, and Clay grasped her other wrist, holding her immobile. She thrashed against him, her hands slipping away from his, fists pounding against his chest and shoulders until he wound his fingers through hers, holding her hands trapped behind her. Clay pulled her against the wall of his chest. Her breath came in short pants. Tears she hadn't realized were falling wet her lips as he held her hostage. She gritted her teeth together, trying not to notice the heat emanating from his body, scorching hers. Regret for the past replaced the anger; need made way for a new kind of agony. She didn't want to feel his thumbs loosen their hold and begin tracing circles against her palms, which were still held behind her back. She didn't want to see the way his eyes had turned dark and hot, pained, and tortured—the same way she felt inside.

"Let me go." Her voice was barely a whisper of sound, an entreaty on a shuddered breath.

"Jen…God, what have I done to us? This wasn't what was supposed to happen."

Her forehead pressed against his chest, her chin tucked down, all fight gone. She was too tired to battle both him and her heart. It was taking every ounce of her strength not to touch her lips to the skin exposed at the neckline of his T-shirt. The scent of him haunted her, making her remember the afternoons by the lake, the nights in one another's arms. She felt his body tense against hers, his belt buckle pressed against her stomach as he walked her backward toward the stall door, her hands still trapped behind her.

She could almost read the thoughts going through his mind. He would let her go but wanted her hands pinned behind her in case she decided to lash out again. How could he not realize that she just wanted to run her hands through his hair and draw his mouth to hers? Couldn't he feel the change in her body, the way she felt it in his?

"I'm so sorry." Clay's forehead fell forward, laying his head against her shoulder, his face turned toward her neck. His breath was hot on her skin, heating her already molten core, making her shiver. "I should have never left you."

His lips brushed against her collarbone as he spoke, and she felt his tears burning against her skin. "It's not what you think. I swear. I'm sorry, Jen. It was never because I didn't love you."

Why was she fighting the feelings she could never hold back? This was Clay. She'd loved him since the first moment she saw him across their corral. She slid her hands from his grasp and curled her fingers into his hair, needing to touch him, offering comfort and forgiveness in her touch. Her arms circled his massive shoulders, her hands playing over the muscles as she stroked him, trying to soothe the raw anguish she could hear in his words and could feel vibrating in his body.

She still didn't know who the woman in the house was, but she knew she couldn't be Clay's wife or girlfriend. He might be a lot of things, but a cheater wasn't one of them. While the cynic in her reminded her not to trust him, her heart beat out a different order: just love him.

He must have finally noticed the change in her because he fell to his knees, his face against her stomach with his arms wrapped around her waist. Jen couldn't still the yearning that pulsed through her veins. She longed for what they had, what she'd *thought* they had, so long ago. Five years was a long time to live with the sting of rejection and abandonment, to erect a wall around her heart to protect herself, and she was sure she'd made it strong enough to withstand anything. Clay's confession, the defeat in his body language, broke through it with the force of a jackhammer, leaving the entire thing in ruins. When he looked up, her hands cupped his face of their own accord, needing to touch him. "Clay," she whispered.

She had no idea what she was about to say but didn't get the chance as he stood and covered her mouth with his own. His lips were gentle, tender, brushing hers as if he were afraid she would disappear. It was a first kiss all over again, filled with hope and longing. It made her heart ache, and her tears fell as it dredged up memories of regret and loss.

She curved her hands around his neck. Now wasn't the time for sweet memories. Later she would allow herself to feel the remorse, the sorrow for what they'd lost. Right now she wanted all of him. She swept her tongue into his mouth and he groaned, his chest rumbling against her. Clay's touch grew desperate as his hands ran up the sides of her ribcage, lifting her shirt from the waistband of her jeans. She clutched at him, knowing if she let him go now, this moment would never return.

Clay's hands—sweet heaven, those calloused hands that drove her mad—slid under her shirt and over her back. She arched against him, the need a physical pain with only one cure. She could feel his erection through his clothing as his arm circled her, holding her flush against him. Every inch of him embraced her, as if she were a missing part of him. His mouth found her throat, and she dropped her head back against the wall, allowing him to take whatever he wanted as long as he wouldn't stop.

"Please," she whispered.

She wasn't even sure what she was begging for but prayed he would figure it out, and quickly. She felt him smile against the flesh of her neck as his hand moved from her back to cup her breast. Brushing aside the thin cotton of her bra, his thumb brushed over the hard peak and she melted, her knees giving way. She would have fallen had he not held her with his own body, pinning her against the wall.

Chapter Seven

CLAY KNEW HE had to stop this. Seeing the anguish in her eyes, the anger fueled by the pain of the past had brought him to his knees. He loved this woman, had always loved her, but leaving had hurt her. And he was about to do it again.

He couldn't stay; Candie's presence was proof of that. If she could track him down here, then her shady creditors could, too, and that was too dangerous. If he didn't stop this now, Jen would hate him even more when he left.

Would that be a bad thing?

Even he had to admit, despising him would make it easier on her when he left. She would be justified in her anger, and her brothers would probably kick his ass before he got down the driveway this time. But in the long run, it would be safer for them all if he took Candie and went as far away as they could.

Right now, his body was rebelling. Every part of him wanted to feel her against him, to have her wrapped around him, enveloping him, holding him. He wanted to bury himself into her, to hear her cry out his name with pleasure instead of spitting it out with hate. As much as he wanted her—and his body throbbed with need—Clay knew he couldn't make love to her and then walk away again, leaving her regretting what only he knew was real. Unfortunately, his body wasn't cooperating with his brain. Instead of taking a step away from her, his hand curved around her breast, his thumb teasing the peak, sending shock waves of electricity through him. His other hand slid down her back, caressing her flesh, the feel of her under his palms making him want more as he tasted her, his mouth finding her throat, her jaw, her lips. The more he touched her, the more lost he became and the less he wanted to listen to the common sense that would protect them both.

He heard the commotion outside before his brain registered the noise at the house. His cell phone vibrated in his pocket. The yelling in the front yard finally broke through the haze of his desire.

"What the hell?" He looked out the barn door over the horse's back to see his sister being dragged from the front porch by two men. "Stay here," he warned, grasping Jen's arms until he saw she understood the seriousness of the situation.

"But, what's—"

"I mean it, Jen. Don't leave this barn for any reason. Get into one of the stalls or lock yourself in the office, and stay there until I come back." He shoved his phone into her hand. "Call the police and tell them to get out here *now*."

"But—"

"Just do it. I'll explain later." He ran a hand over her cheek and wished he had time to tell her everything. *Please don't let anyone find her in here.*

Clay ran out the back of the barn, wishing they were back in Texas where he had a concealed weapon permit. Here in California, he was just going to have to hope his brains and his fists would be enough of a defense to keep everyone safe.

He didn't recognize the two men dragging Candie by her arms to a large SUV. The smaller of the two was skinny but looked wiry. While he appeared to be calling the shots, Clay was more concerned with the other man, who was a match for him size-wise and looked like the muscle of the operation. This situation screamed danger, and he wasn't sure whether to make his presence known or to use the element of surprise.

His gaze snapped to the porch as Scott and Derek bolted from the front door. Scott was leveling a shotgun at the men. "Let her go!" he yelled.

Clay had never been more grateful for his friend. While Scott distracted the pair, Clay moved behind the corral, circling to the back of the black SUV he'd been too preoccupied to hear arriving. He ducked by its back tire.

"Put it down, cowboy, or we'll kill her." The muscle wound an arm around Candie's neck, making her look like a gazelle in the jaws of a lion.

Scott lowered the gun to his side.

"Smart move. Get her in the car," Skinny ordered his partner. "We'll send someone back to deal with them later."

"Stop it, D. You know I don't like it rough." His sister's smart mouth never ceased to amaze Clay. He watched as she tried to break Muscle's grasp on her, but he twisted her arm higher on her back, between her shoulder blades, until she yelped in pain as he pushed her toward the vehicle. Clay prayed Mike and Silvie wouldn't come back from town until after the police arrived.

Please let the police get here soon.

Muscle-man shoved Candie against the driver's side of the car, and Clay heard her grunt of pain. "I was just on my way to see you guys."

"Get in. Unless you want to see your friends dead, quit jabbering and go where we want you to go."

"I told you I was coming to get your money. You didn't even give me time to get it."

Clay prayed his sister was playing a role for these thugs. He didn't want to believe she would have conned him for money, but it wouldn't be the first time if she had. He squatted at the back bumper of the SUV, still hidden from view, trying to figure out a way to stall the two thugs until the police arrived. The ranch was a ways out of town, and these two could be long gone before the cops even realized the severity of the situation. He felt the folding knife in his pocket jam against his hipbone. If he could cut the wall of the tire deep enough to flatten it without notice, they wouldn't get far. He pulled the knife out and opened it.

He saw Muscle-man grab his sister by the cheeks with one massive-sized hand. "You're not that good a con, sweets." The man laughed, but there was no humor in the sound. "Now you can dance at the club to pay your debt."

"Just get her into the car!" Skinny gave the order and opened the back door of the SUV.

Clay knew he didn't have time to waste. He wiggled the pocket knife against the wall of the tire, easing it through the rubber before moving forward to the passenger door. He had to hurry up if he wanted to get away before they noticed him. The SUV shifted as Candie was forcefully shoved into the back and Muscle-man climbed in after her.

Skinny started the engine and Clay backpedaled away from the car, intent on getting behind the shrubs that lined the corral near the driveway. He dove behind the brush, knowing that Scott and Derek had to have seen him but praying the two men hadn't. Now, if he could just get Jen into the house safely.

"What the..." The door of the SUV slammed, and Clay glanced over his shoulder in time to see Skinny come around the front of the vehicle to see the rapidly flattening tire. "Get her out!" He gave the order as he looked around the premises for the culprit.

He turned to Scott, pulling out his handgun. "Give me the keys to the truck."

"No." Scott lifted the shotgun to his shoulder.

"Look, we don't want any trouble from you. We have what we came for."

Skinny gestured toward Candie with his gun as the other man dragged her out of the car.

"Let her go," Scott repeated, his voice steady.

Clay couldn't leave Scott to handle these guys. He glanced back at the barn and saw Jen edging out of the office into the aisleway. If he could see her, so could the men. Damn if she didn't look ready to take them on, too. He had to do something before they spotted her. Without caring about the consequences, Clay moved out from his hiding place and stepped onto the driveway.

"Here. Take mine." Both men spun, dragging Candie with them, as they turned toward Clay. Candie's eyes widened, and he saw something in his sister's eyes he'd never seen before: fear. "Take my truck; it's yours, but let her go."

Clay saw the flash of greed in Skinny's eyes. "Which one?"

He had the man's attention now and wondered how much money his sister owed this guy. Not that it mattered. If it kept her safe, kept them from noticing Jen in the barn, and left Scott and Derek unharmed, they could have the truck. No amount of money was worth his family in jeopardy.

"Black dually." He reached into his pocket, eyeing the pair suspiciously and jingled the keys. "We trade the truck for her."

"Take the truck," Muscle-man whispered loudly. "It's worth way more than she owes."

"Shut up." Skinny shoved him, never taking his eyes off Clay. "Toss me the keys."

"Let her go first."

"You get her, and we leave with no trouble?"

Clay held his hands into the air. "You're the one with the gun, man."

Scott slid the gun to his side as Skinny uncocked the pistol, put it into his jacket, and shoved Candie toward Clay. "Keys." It wasn't a request.

Clay tossed the keys Skinny's way before catching his sister as she stumbled against him and guiding her back to the house. The two men ran for the truck, jumping inside. Clay was grateful for the "honor among thieves" mentality of these criminals as he urged Scott to get everyone inside. He could just hear sirens in the distance and knew, if those guys heard them, too, they were dead. He wasn't taking any chances with Jen still in the barn.

JEN WATCHED FROM the window of the office in the barn as Clay stood off with the two men, unable to breathe until she saw the gun concealed again. When Clay tossed his keys and rushed Candie back to the house, she wondered if everyone was just going to leave her alone in the barn. She was certain she'd convinced the police dispatcher that this was an emergency, but she had no idea how long it was going to take. Each second seemed to take an eternity to tick by. Clay's truck had barely backed up and started down the driveway, spraying gravel, when she heard the first sirens in the distance. When either of those two realized someone had called the police, they'd be worse off than when this whole mess first started. She wasn't about to leave Clay out there alone to deal with those men when they came back.

She left the office, running into the aisle and heading for the front of the barn. She didn't care that the men might see her. She just knew she had to warn Clay, make sure he was safe in the house as well.

"Jennifer, get back inside."

She spun at his voice, seeing him in the back of the barn, relief flooding her as she ran toward him, throwing herself into his arms. "Clay, the police should be here any second, but if those guys see—"

"They'll come after us. So, get inside." He pushed her back into the office. She hurried to the window, barely able to make out the truck through the trees blocking her vantage point. It looked like it was stopped halfway down the driveway.

"They must have heard the sirens," she told him. The truck peeled out; this time backing up, heading for the house again. "They're coming back, Clay."

"Give me my phone." She handed him back his cell phone from her pocket, and he punched buttons quickly. She saw him pause before texting again. "Okay, Candie is inside with your brothers. They're calling the police so Scott can tell the officers that these guys are armed and heading back toward the house." He stepped behind her, looking out the window with her as several police cruisers sped down the driveway, dust swirling around the cars and blocking the thugs from view. They watched as cruisers followed the truck to the front of the house, surrounding it, waiting for the men to exit.

"Stay here," Clay breathed into her ear. He turned to leave the office.

"What? No!" she yelled, following him. There was no way she was letting him get out of her sight again. Those men had pulled a gun, and she wasn't taking any chance of losing him. "Either I go with you or we both stay."

"Fine." He pulled her back inside the doorway. "We stay." He leaned his head around the door, watching the standoff.

The pair, realizing their chance at freedom was gone, exited the truck and were immediately shoved to the ground and cuffed. Jennifer tried to edge past Clay to get a good look, but he kept pressing her behind him. This protector thing was getting a bit out of hand.

"Will you move? I want to see."

He turned his head slowly and looked at her as if she had just grown a third eyeball. "Are you *nuts*?" Clay held both of her arms and moved her against the wall, pressing his own body against hers so she couldn't get past him. "This is serious, Jen. Not a television show. Those are real guns."

"And you were stupid enough to put yourself right in the line of fire." She shoved against his chest. "You could've gotten yourself killed."

"It's better than *you* getting killed. Now stay here while I go talk to the police." She watched as he walked toward the house, leaving her in the barn alone again.

"I don't think so," she muttered, following him.

He spun on her. "Get inside."

"Freeze!" Jen stopped midstride, her eyes growing wide as no less than three very serious looking officers turned toward them, with weapons leveled. "Put your hands up and get on your knees."

"What? I live here. I'm the one who called—"

"I said, on your knees!" Several more officers moved toward them, triangulating their positions as two peeled away and edged closer.

"Jen, shut up and get on your knees." She glanced back toward Clay who was already on his knees with his hands folded on top of his head like he was a criminal in a movie.

She copied him, dropping to her knees and raising her hands on top of her head. "This is ridiculous, I…ow!" She yelped as an officer rushed and twisted her arm behind her back, cuffing her wrists.

This was *not* the way she'd envisioned this standoff ending.

JEN SAT ON the front porch, absently rubbing at her wrists where the handcuffs had pinched. It didn't take long for the officers to realize who was actually involved and who belonged in the back of squad cars once they were able to start inquiring. Luckily, nothing more than her pride had been injured.

She wished she could sit everyone down the way the police did and get some answers to her questions. Like who Candie was, why those men showed up at her house, and how all of this involved Clay enough for him to sacrifice his truck, if not his life, to save Candie. He was still upstairs with Candie, where he'd been for the last hour after the police left, and he wasn't letting anyone else close to her. She didn't like his secrecy, and if he thought he was going to stay in their home, especially after what just happened, he was going to give her some answers, whether he wanted to or not.

"You look like you've got a lot on your mind."

Jen couldn't help but be a bit disappointed to see her brother instead of Clay. "This is crazy, Scott. Has he told you anything?"

"Just what I already knew." Scott shrugged and shook his head sympathetically. "He didn't know this would happen, Jen. Candie showing up, those guys, the police… none of it was his fault."

"I know *that*." She sighed and let her hands fall into her lap as she stared out toward the corral. "Who is Candie, really?"

"She's my sister."

Both of them turned toward the doorway at the sound of Clay's voice. Scott rose quickly. "I should let the two of you talk. I think it's long overdue." The pointed look he shot Clay didn't escape her notice.

Clay gave him an apologetic look, and Jennifer wondered how much Scott had been keeping from her. She watched her brother slink out of the room before she could pin him down with questions.

"My half-sister," Clay clarified, taking a seat next to her. "The youngest of the three of us."

"Three?" Clay had never opened up about his family before, and she wasn't sure what she could ask now without him clamming up again.

He nodded. "I'm the oldest. My brother, Bobby, over-dosed, and Candie is the youngest. I promised my mother before she died that I'd take care of her. Candie came looking for me when she got into trouble again. Those men were here because she owed them money. I don't know whether it was for drugs or some con job she did, and she's not telling me now."

Jennifer shook her head, staring at her hands as she tried to put the pieces together into some semblance of the life she'd never known he faced. Angry tears burned at the back of her eyes for pain he'd gone through, for the things he'd never shared with her, for the life they could have had. "I don't even know what to say, Clay. I'm so sorry about your brother and your mother. Why didn't you ever tell me?"

"I ran away from all of it a long time ago, at my mother's request." He rubbed his hands on his thighs, unable to hide what she now recognized as fear in his eyes. His voice was agonized, and she could see the need to escape making him fidget. "She wanted me to get away from all of this. What she didn't know was it's like a demon that won't let go."

"But you're not…" She wasn't sure what to say. He was a different man than the one she'd known five years ago. She didn't know anything about him now, if she ever really knew him at all; she had only seen what he allowed her to see.

"No, I'm not an addict." He ran his fingers through his hair. "As a kid, I started selling for some older guys in high school. Mom wanted me out of that life, wanted all of us out of it, but I was the only one who escaped. When

I came here, you and Mike helped me forget about my past, until Mom called again and needed me."

The tears she couldn't hold back any longer slipped down her cheek unchecked. Suddenly, it was beginning to make sense.

Clay reached for her hand, his thumb tracing circles over her palm, but he wouldn't look at her face. "Jen, I didn't want to leave. It nearly killed me. When Mom called to tell me about Bobby...she begged me to find a way to save Candie. Mom was dying from cancer." He shook his head. "Maybe if I'd stayed, things would've been different. I could have kept Candie safe, kept Bobby alive. I could have—"

"No, you don't know how it would have turned out," she interrupted him, dropping to her knees between his thighs, cupping his face between her palms. She couldn't bear to imagine him in place of his brother, dead from an overdose. "Why didn't you ever tell me any of this?"

His gaze finally met hers. "What could I say? My druggie family is falling apart, and I need to go take care of them?" He rubbed his temples with his fingers. "Jen, look what happened today. You or your brothers could have been killed. I couldn't live with myself if something happened to you."

Reality struck her in the chest, freezing the blood in her veins. If he thought he'd protected her the first time by leaving, he might run in order to protect her again. He slipped his hands down to cover hers, and she began to tremble. "Clay, please?" She wasn't sure what she was asking for, but she could see the resignation in his eyes.

"Jen." His voice was tender as his thumb traced her cheekbone. "God, I love you. I've thought about you every day, wished things could have been different for us." He brushed away a tear with his thumb.

"They still can be. Your leaving didn't stop anything. You can't run away from your past, but if you face it…"

"This happened *because* I came back." His voice was husky, agonized and sorrowful. "I can't stay."

"Clay," she began, but he stopped her with a finger to her lips.

"This will keep happening. I have to take care of Candie, but I won't put you in danger doing it."

In that moment, she knew his mind was made up. He was certain he was putting her in harm's way. Clay would go to the ends of the earth to protect her and her family, even if it meant hurting both of them in the process. Regardless of what she said to convince him it wasn't true, he was too stubborn to believe anything to the contrary. He was leaving again, and her heart was about to be ripped out. It wasn't as much an *if* as it was a *when*. Unless she could prove him wrong.

"Then just stay tonight."

The words tumbled from her lips before she could stop them. Not that she really wanted to. Clay was the only man she'd ever loved, and although she'd tried to lie to herself, she'd never stopped. He'd been with her, in her heart, every day since the night he left. If one more night was all she could have of him, she was going to cast aside the past and ignore the future to have this one brief moment in the present with him.

"Stay with me tonight." Her eyes met his, pleading without words, before she brushed her lips against his. "Please, I promise I won't ask for more."

"You do still owe me a dinner," he whispered against her mouth. He tried to laugh, to force a bit of humor into his voice, but his eyes were sad, already resigned to the decision he'd made. "Go get ready, and I'll take you out for the best dinner of your life."

Chapter Eight

"YOU ARE THE biggest idiot on the face of the earth!" As usual, Candie didn't hold anything back. It didn't matter that she was to blame for the mess he was in; she was going to rip him a new one whether he deserved it or not.

"I really don't need this now, Candie." Clay's voice was a low growl.

"Mom did *not* tell you to give up your life just so you can be a martyr pretending to save me from some non-existent danger."

"Yeah, well, those guys today seemed pretty real to me." He brushed past her and reached for a clean Western shirt he hoped Jen would like. "And that gun…yeah, it got real when it was pointed your way."

Clay wasn't sure if Candie had been eavesdropping on him with Jen earlier or if she'd just happened to hear their conversation, but she wasn't letting the subject drop, and it was grating on his last already raw nerve. He wanted to enjoy this night with Jen, not spend their limited time regretting his promise to his mother any more than he already did. However, Candie was making it pretty hard not to regret it right now.

"I don't need you to take care of me. I'm doing just fine on my own."

Clay held up a folded wad of cash between his fingers "So, you don't need this then? And those guys weren't coming to collect on some deal you ran out on?" He tossed the money onto the bedspread, trying to hide his aversion to his sister's lifestyle choices. His already short fuse was getting shorter by the second.

Candie rose from the side of his bed and stared down at the money scattered over the comforter. "You know what, Clay? If I'd realized how much you were throwing away, I never would have asked for your help. I won't be the reason you walk away from her."

Clay sighed, feeling like a judgmental jerk as he scooped up the money and held it out toward his sister. "Just take the money, Candie. Pay off whatever debts are hanging over your head and clean up your act. Get a real job, something."

She huffed and shook her head at him. "I don't want your money, Clay. I *have* money." She held up a wad of cash twice the size of his. "I wanted your help. I wanted you to help me get on my feet somewhere near you so we could finally be a family without all the running and hiding. I didn't owe D money. He was mad because I refused to hustle for him anymore." She repocketed her money.

"And, so we're clear, I am drug free. I haven't touched anything since I got clean two years ago."

"You said you owed the guy who fixed your car."

"I said I stiffed him. He tried to charge me for repairs he never made. But thanks for your vote of confidence. It's refreshing."

"Candie." Clay followed her out the bedroom door. "Can you blame me?"

"I guess not," she conceded. "But from the sounds of things, you've been blaming me for your being a coward for at least five years now. I'm not going to be your scapegoat. I'll call you and let you know where I land." She turned her back on him as she marched down the stairs. "Until then, get your head out of your ass and marry that woman. Although, God only knows why she wants you."

Still shirtless, Clay followed her down the stairs. "You're not going to land anywhere except on your ass, Candie. I've heard this before." He watched his sister walk out the front door, ignoring him. "Until the police called," he added. "Candie!" Within minutes, he heard the sound of her run-down car chugging to a start. Without answering him, she backed up and headed down the driveway, leaving behind a cloud of smelly exhaust and his frustration. Candie had a way of breezing in and out of his life, like a hurricane—without warning, amassing nothing but destruction in her wake. Now what was he supposed to do?

JEN STEPPED ONTO the front porch as Clay tipped his glass of water back and took a quick swallow. As soon as he saw her, his eyes grew wide and he started to cough, spitting the water onto her brother seated across from him.

"Nice, Clay," Derek said, flipping his drenched hands in front of him. "That was smooth." Derek looked at her. "Are you sure you *want* to go to dinner with him? He might spill a beer down the front of you for all the class he's got."

Clay glared at him. "Sorry, I just…"

His gaze traveled from her hair, piled on her head in a loose, messy bun, to the dress that hugged every curve while actually showing very little skin. She'd found it on a clearance rack and wondered where she'd ever wear it with its loose, draped neckline and sleeves with shoulder cutouts. It hit midthigh, and with a pair of black, knee-high boots, it was dressy and casual simultaneously.

"Wow. Just…wow!" Clay took her hand and led her toward his truck.

She blushed under his appreciative glance. "You did say to dress up."

"Don't worry, Jen, we won't wait up for you," Derek called, making her blush again as Clay opened the door for her.

"You look nice, Clay," she murmured, her hand on his forearm as she climbed into the truck. She was careful to hold her dress to her thighs, but it rode up higher than she'd thought it would, giving Clay a glimpse of most of her leg. She heard him groan quietly as he closed the door.

He climbed into the driver's side and looked at her again, fumbling with his key. "You make me want to skip dinner and go right to dessert."

She ignored the burning sensation on her cheeks. She'd heard the angry voices and Candie's hasty departure and worried Clay might cancel their date altogether. She didn't want to get her hopes up that he might stay, but just in case he only stayed tonight, she wanted to make the most of every second. Her stomach was so twisted in knots that she didn't think she'd be able to eat anyway.

"We could."

She saw him close his eyes and inhale deeply, before turning his hot gaze on her again. "Woman, you're killing me. I promised you dinner, and we are going to dinner." His voice scolded, but she could see the hint of a smile at the corner of his lips.

She could also see the tension in his shoulders melt away as he pulled the truck onto the main road before turning onto the highway. There weren't many cars on the road, but it was a weeknight and most people would be heading to bed. Early mornings didn't lend well to late-night dates when everyone had to get up at the crack of dawn to feed animals.

As much as she hated the travel rodeo forced on her, she couldn't imagine doing anything else. It allowed her to work with her family from their home, doing what they loved with nothing but wide-open spaces surrounding her. Something no other job could offer. She looked back at Clay and wondered if he was doing what he wanted. His hands twisted around the steering wheel, squeaking on the leather in the quiet of the truck. He gripped it hard enough to turn his knuckles white.

"You okay?" she asked.

"You're wearing my favorite perfume." His voice was deep and husky, like he'd just woken from a long night's sleep. She watched as he took a turn she hadn't expected.

"Aren't we going to dinner?" There was nothing down this road but a few small farms and Mills River Dude Ranch.

"I called in a favor; Jerry Mills rented me one of his cabins." Her heart skidded to a stop before pounding out of control. A cabin?

He turned toward her. "I'm having dinner delivered."

Like ice cream in the summer sun, her body seemed to be melting on the spot at the mere thought of being alone with him. Not wanting him to know she was nothing more than a puddle of desire, she sought out her mischievous side. "It's not pizza, is it? Because I'd hate to think I got this dressed up for pepperoni."

He laughed. God, how she'd missed him.

"No, but it *is* a surprise, so you'll have to wait and see."

CLAY PULLED UP to the cabin and silently thanked Jerry for making this happen. Leaving Jen in the truck, he went into the cabin and lit several candles around the room, including two tapers on the small dining table. He removed the food from the delivery plates and put them on the dinnerware Jerry had left out for him. If it weren't so hot, he would have lit a fire. He looked at the romantic setting of the room and sighed at the bittersweet irony.

Now that he'd finally opened up and been honest with Jen, she wanted him to stay. But it hadn't changed anything. She would always be in danger with him.

Even though Candie swore she'd be fine, until he knew for sure, he couldn't take her word for it. He'd heard it before. And, with her ignoring his calls, he had no idea where she'd driven off to in that hunk of junk she drove; therefore, he wasn't holding out much hope.

He hurried back to where Jen waited for him, with her door open and facing out. Clay took her hand, but she pulled him back toward her. His hand immediately fell to her thigh, unable to stand close without touching her.

"Look, a shooting star." She pointed up.

The movement closed the distance between them. Clay's body heated, and he felt the blood throb in his veins. He looked down at her, grateful for the darkness that would hide every feeling he knew was on his face at that moment. "Make a wish, Jen." He almost choked on emotion as he said the words.

She looked up at him and laid a hand against his chest. He was sure she could feel his heart racing beneath her fingers. "I already did."

He wanted to ask what it was, whether it was about him, or better yet *them*, but fear gripped his lungs and kept him from speaking. He couldn't help but make his own wish in that moment—that their circumstances were different, that he wouldn't have to leave when the sun came up. He cleared his throat, ruining the moment, and led her inside the cabin. As he held her chair, she just stared at him. Damn, his fool stubborn pride. Why couldn't he just tell her what he was thinking? What he was feeling?

"You don't want to know what it was?" In the candle-light, her eyes looked as if they were lit by a fire within.

"Jen, let's just hold onto what we have tonight." He didn't want to think past this moment, this night, because that would lead him down the road to leaving again, to the day when Candie came back looking for more money or for him to bail her out of trouble again.

She smiled softly and rose from her seat, moving to stand beside him, laying her hand on his cheek. "Then let's have dessert before dinner after all. It's not *tonight* I want to hold." Without another word, she turned her back to him and walked toward the small cabin's bedroom. "Coming?" she asked, glancing at him over her shoulder before disappearing.

Clay sighed. Jen was tempting him more than he thought was possible. He rubbed his hands on his thighs, hating himself for giving in when he should be walking away. With his fingers tugging at the knot of his tie, he followed her into the room. His phone vibrated in his pocket; he thought about ignoring it, but he was still worried about where Candie had headed to, driving that hunk-of-junk. *Please don't let her be stranded on the side of the road needing me to pick her up now. I don't know that I could force myself to leave.*

He glanced at the screen and saw the text: *At my Dad's with his new wife in Truckee. Going to work in her hair salon. All is good (I promise), so marry her already.*

Clay let out a long breath of relief that she'd arrived some place in one piece. Honestly, of all the men his mother had been involved with, Candie's father had been his favorite. His sister, like their mother, had a wild streak, but if anyone else was going to be able to help Candie get her life back on track, it was her father. Now that Candie had finally decided to clean up her act, the small tourist town in the Sierras might be just the secluded place for her to get a fresh start.

He tapped the keys on his phone, texting her back with the only important question when it came to his flighty sister: *How long are you staying?*

The reply was immediate: *Until I come back for your wedding. I'm safe, I promise.*

Despite all of the ways Candie had messed up over the years, she had her stubborn pride, and she never *ever* went back on a promise. This was her way of letting him know he should move on with his life; she was releasing him from his promise to their mother by doing the most difficult thing she could—staying out of trouble. A smile curved his mouth as he texted her back: *Love you, little sister. Wedding will be ASAP.*

Clay looked back toward the bedroom and grinned. The woman in there had no idea what was about to happen.

IF SOMEONE HAD told Jen a week ago that she'd be lying in a cabin, trying to seduce Clayton Graham into staying with her, she'd have laughed in his face. As a matter of fact, she probably would have punched him in the mouth. Yet here she was, lying in nothing more than a see-through wisp of a bra, a lace thong, and garters, no less, hoping to convince him to give them another chance. She'd never been a good flirt, and this was so far beyond her realm of expertise. She felt like a fool, an *exposed* fool. Especially since he hadn't followed her into the room. The more time that passed, the more she wondered if she shouldn't give up this pursuit altogether. She glanced at the empty doorway again.

You're an idiot, Jennifer.

She rose and reached for her dress at the foot of the bed, turning her back to the doorway and slipping it back over her head.

"What did I miss?"

She heard Clay's husky laughter as her arms were caught over her head, twisted in the dress she was now regretting. She quickly tugged at the dress, but it wouldn't cooperate. "I was…I just…"

His grin widened, causing the dimple in his cheek to deepen. "I think I liked it better the way it was."

She glared at him with the only eye visible through the neckline of her dress. One minute he was pushing her away, the next, pulling her closer. She was getting whiplash from his mood swings.

"Yeah? Well, you missed your chance, pal. I'm done playing games." Jen finally maneuvered her dress down and bent over to pull on her boots.

Clay's hands found the curve of her bottom and slid over her hip to her waist, urging her back to standing before she got the boot on. "No games. Nothing between us but the past, and we need to talk about it for a second." Her breath caught in her throat, blocking any of the retorts she might think of. "I was an idiot to ever leave you. I wanted to protect you from my past and the trouble that seemed to follow me wherever I went. All I did was hurt you myself. I thought if you saw where I came from, *what* I came from, you'd leave." He held her chin between his thumb and finger. "I'm sorry for being a fool, for being afraid to let you see the real me. For not trusting what we had."

His eyes grew dark, the green deepening. "I love you, Jennifer Chandler. I always have and I always will, but I can't hurt you anymore. I can't stand to see that pain in your eyes, the fear that I'm going to leave you—like your parents, like I did before."

Tears filled her eyes, washing away the desire she'd felt only moments ago, leaving agony in its wake. This was how it would happen. This was how he would walk away again, and this time, she wouldn't be able to find all the broken pieces of her heart.

He moved forward, cupping her face in his hands and bending his head until his lips barely brushed hers. "Marry me?"

Her heart stopped completely, and she wondered if she might pass out. "What?"

She tried to pull away from him, to see his face, but he wouldn't allow it. His mouth found hers, his tongue sweeping inside, caressing, teasing, and toying with her. She wanted answers, to know if she'd actually heard him right, but he had other plans. His hands plunged into her hair as his lips continued to demand her all. Jen pressed her palms against his chest, but instead of pushing him away as her brain instructed, her hands slid over the muscles tensing under her touch. Clay groaned deep in his throat and pulled back, pressing his forehead against hers.

"Say yes." His hands moved over her ribs, his thumbs brushing along the curve of her breasts. "Say you'll marry me, already." Barely restraining himself, his fingers clenched along her sides. One hand reached into his pants pocket, and he withdrew the diamond solitaire he'd given her so long ago. "Be my wife, and I promise I will never go anywhere again."

The diamond glinted in the near darkness, catching light from down the hall and winking at her. "I thought you couldn't stay." A tremor of fear rippled through her. What if she said yes and he was gone again in the morning? Would he leave her the next time Candie needed him?

"I was wrong," he said between kisses, nibbling at her lips. "So wrong. Marry me, Jen."

"Clay, I thought you…"

"I know what you thought, what I let you think, but Candie is safe, at least for now, and she forced me to face a few things. The most important thing was that I can't lose you again. Nothing is more important than you."

As if sensing her hesitation, he smiled. "I'm staying whether you say yes or no, so you might as well agree now. Otherwise it's going to be damn uncomfortable for us when we're working together at the ranch." She laughed even through her tears. "You know," he began, his eyes glinting with playful hunger, "the sooner you say yes, the sooner we can get this dress off again, and I can see if you are really wearing that garter belt I thought I saw."

"I should make you sweat a while after what you've put me through." She knew she wouldn't.

"Trust me, Jen." His eyes stared into hers with a heat like molten lava, melting every bone in her body and making everything south of her waist throb with yearning. "I'm sweating."

His hand brushed the shoulder of her dress to the side, and his lips found the edge of her collarbone. A jolt of electricity shot over her shoulders and down her spine as his hands slid back up her sides to tease the peak of her breast through her clothing. One hand moved to curve around her hip, pressing her against his straining erection.

"And aching," he murmured against the side of her throat. "Say yes," he repeated as he ran his tongue over the hollow just below her ear. "Marry me." His lips trailed over her jaw as her head fell back.

His fingers gripped her rear. "I'm still waiting, Jen." He reached for her hand, holding the ring at the end of her finger.

"Yes," she whispered, laughing through her tears. "But, so help me," she warned, sliding her free hand to the front of his pants. "If you even think of leaving me a second time, you'll never ride right again."

Clay slid his calloused hands up her thighs, letting the dress rise with his hand to her waist. "Trust me; this is exactly where I want to be. And I'm going to spend every day proving it to you, starting right now."

Epilogue

JENNIFER PRESSED THE bowl of potato salad into Clay's hands. "Here, put this out for me? I know it's your favorite." She gave him a wicked grin, thinking about the bowl she'd dumped on his head not too long ago.

"Don't give me that look. You wouldn't dare dump this on me because you know I'll smear wedding cake on your face without thinking twice," he said, sliding the bowl onto the kitchen table before returning to her side.

"Let's not start a food fight." She laughed, feeling completely overwhelmed with adoration for her husband of only four hours.

Clay reached for her waist and drew her into his embrace, pressing her back against the kitchen countertop. "Only if we have a private food fight and I get to pick the foods. I'm thinking some ice cream, caramel syrup…" His eyes gleamed mischievously as she smacked his bicep.

"You're sort of incorrigible. You know that, right?"

Clay's fingers trailed up the sides of her wedding dress and over the curved sweetheart neckline, sending shivers of warm heat spiraling to her core, making her anxious to leave for their honeymoon.

"You know it's just one of the many things you love about me."

"Yes," she agreed, pressing a quick kiss to his lips. "And because you're so charismatic." Clay drew back and looked at her quizzically. "Scott told me all about how you were sure you could get me to forgive you. Guess I wasn't as easy as you thought."

"It was all part of my plan." He ran his thumb over her cheekbone, growing serious. "How long do you want to stay? Our flight isn't until nine tonight."

"I want you all to myself as soon as possible," she answered, curling her arm around his waist. "But I want you to have plenty of time to visit with your sister."

"I forgot to tell you, but Candie asked about staying with us for a few weeks after she finishes school next summer. I think she's debating settling down in a small town now that she's had a taste of it."

"She's moving here?" Jen was surprised. After talking for the past several months on the phone and video chat, Clay and his sister were finally coming to terms with their past mistakes and putting them where they belonged—in the past. Candie not only managed to stay out of trouble but went back to school to get her cosmetology license. When she arrived a few days before the wedding, Jen had barely recognized the blond who walked up the porch stairs. She was beautiful, healthy, and, more important than anything else, happy and worry free. Deep down, Jen and Clay had both been worried that Candie would bore of small town living and go back to her old ways. Seeing the change in her made Jen's joy complete.

"She's thinking about it. Probably about the same time Derek graduates and comes home. It would be a full house." He glanced through the kitchen window at the crowd of people milling around the food tables and near the makeshift dance floor they'd set up in the yard. "Would you mind?"

She cupped the smooth surface of his fresh shaven cheek, missing his usual five o'clock shadow. "Clayton Michael Graham," she scolded. "Your family is my family. She can move in whenever she wants to. We'll make it work." She smiled at him. "Candie and I were talking about chopping off this mop I call hair. It would be nice to have a stylist around."

Clay ran his hands through her long, curled tresses, cupping the back of her head. "Don't you dare." He bent forward and nibbled at the corner of her mouth. "Are you sure you're okay with her staying here? Just until she gets on her feet."

"More than okay, happy about it." Jen curled her hand around the back of his neck and pressed her lips against his.

"You know, Jerry gave me a key to one of the cabins, in case we wanted to leave early tonight. We could make a stop before the airport."

Her brows knit on her forehead and she frowned. "We can't run away. The band hasn't even started yet." She laughed at his eagerness to get her alone.

"Not run away. This time I'm running toward something—our future, together." He tipped her chin up so that their eyes met. "I love you, Jennifer. I might run, but it will be forward, with your hand in mine, forever."

Clay kissed her, holding her against his body, making her forget the hundreds of family and friends waiting for them in the yard. She clung to him, letting her body melt against his frame, letting her love for him overflow. Somehow, her cowboy had found his way back home, pushing aside the pain and regret of the past to embrace the future.

"Eh-hem."

Jennifer turned and looked at the kitchen door where Mike stood, smiling broadly. "Go away, Mike." Clay teased the older man, but his eyes never left Jen's face. "You're interrupting."

"Yeah, well, I guess that's my prerogative since I'm the one responsible for your having such a lovely wife." He pulled several serving trays of food from the refrigerator. "We have hungry guests waiting to toast the bride and groom again."

Clay sighed and hung his head. "Fine, let's go make yet another appearance before we steal away for the night."

He wasn't fooling her. She caught Clay's grin as he led her toward the doorway. Jen paused long enough to embrace Mike. "Thank you," she whispered.

Mike smiled down at her, his eyes gleaming with parental pride. "I was thrilled to walk you down the aisle today."

"Thank you for giving me back what I hadn't realized I missed." She kissed Mike's cheek.

"You're very welcome, kiddo. Sometimes you've got to let that pony run, and other times, you need to just lead him where he needs to be."

Acknowledgments

WITH EVERY BOOK I write, it seems like I have more people to thank. I have made some of my best friends during the writing of this series, both traditionally published and indie authors. I want to especially thank the Avon ladies (you guys know who you are!) for setting the bar high and pushing me to get better with each and every book I write. You are the most amazingly talented group of authors a girl could ask for as mentors.

A huge thank you to the Avon Addicts! Without you, I would still be floundering in my bubble of self-doubt midway through my second story. You are my coffee and pump me up to write daily.

I must thank my amazingly talented editor, Rebecca, who made this manuscript shine and made edits painless and fun. Without you, I'd be an OCD mess right now.

Thank-you hugs and kisses go all around to my family and husband. You have put up with so many months of fix-your-own dinners, group house cleaning sessions, and "Shh, mom's got the headphones on" days in the past year just to help me reach my dreams. I love you guys to the moon and back again.

And to the One who makes all of this possible, thank you! I am so very blessed that I still pinch myself when I wake.

Continue reading for an excerpt from

LEARNING THE ROPES

by T. J. Kline

Available now from Avon Impulse!

An Excerpt from

LEARNING THE ROPES

Chapter One

ALICIA KANANI SLAPPED the reins against her horse's rump as he stretched out, practically flying between the barrels down the length of the rodeo arena, dirt clods kicking up behind them as the paint gelding ate up the ground with his long stride. She glanced at the clock as she pulled him up, circling to slow him to a jog as a cowboy opened the back gate, allowing her to exit. 16.45. It was good enough for only second place right now. *Damn it!* If only she'd been able to cut the first barrel closer, it might have taken another tenth of a second off her time.

She walked her favorite gelding, Beast, back to the trailer and hooked the halter around his neck before loosening his cinch. The titter of female laughter floated on the breeze, and recognition dawned as the pair of women moved from behind her trailer. Alicia cringed.

"Look, Dallas, there's Miss Runner Up." Delilah jerked her chin at Alicia's trailer. "Came in second again, huh?" She flipped her long blond waves over her shoulder. "I guess you can't win them all...oh, wait," she giggled. "You don't seem to win any, do you? That would be me." The pair laughed as if it were the funniest joke ever.

"Isn't it hard to ride a broom *and* a horse at the same time, Delilah?" Alicia tipped her head to the side innocently as Delilah glared at her and stormed away, dragging Dallas with her.

Delilah had been a thorn in her side ever since high school when Alicia first arrived in West Hills. There'd never been a lack of competition between them but, years later, only one of them had matured at all.

Alicia snidely imitated Delilah's laugh to her horse as she pulled the saddle from his back and put it into the back of the trailer. "She thinks she's so funny. 'You haven't won, I have,'" she mimicked in a nasally voice. "What a bitch," she muttered as she rubbed the curry comb over Beast's neck and back.

"I sure hope you don't kiss your mother with that mouth."

"Chris!" Alicia spun to see Chris Thomas, her best friend Sydney's brother, walking toward her trailer. She hurried over and gave him a bear hug. "Did you rope already?"

"Later tonight, during the slack. Too many entries, so hopefully we finish before the barbecue starts."

She'd rodeoed with Chris and Sydney for years until Chris had gone pro with his team roping partner. For the last few years, they'd all been pursuing the same goal, the National Finals Rodeo in their events. So far their paths hadn't crossed since Sydney's wedding nearly two years ago. She'd suspected she might see him here since they were so close to home and this particular rodeo boasted a huge purse for team ropers. Her eyes did a quick survey of him, realizing the past couple of years had been very good to him. Unfortunately, he had always oozed self-confidence and she was sure he was aware of the fact.

"I see Delilah's still giving you a hard time."

She shrugged and gave him a half-smile. "She's still mad I beat her out for rodeo queen when Sydney gave up the title."

"That was a long time ago. You'd think she'd let it go." Chris stuffed one hand into his pockets and leaned against the side of her trailer, patting Beast's neck. "Maybe you should put Nair in her shampoo like she did to you."

Alicia cringed at the memory. "Ugh! It was a good thing I smelled it before I put it on my head. That could've been traumatic. But I got her back."

Chris laughed out loud. "Didn't you put liniment in her lip gloss?"

She pinched her lips together, trying to keep from laughing at the reminder of the prank. They had some good times together in the past. She wondered how they'd managed to drift apart over the past few years. She missed his laugh and the way he always seemed to bring the playful side of her personality to the surface. One minute they were traveling together, the three of them inseparable, and the next they hadn't spoken more than a few words in years.

"So, how'd you do?" he asked.

"Second, so far. Again," she clarified.

Chris gave her a lopsided grin and crossed his arms over his chest. She tried not to notice how his biceps bulged against the material of his Western shirt or how much he'd filled out since she'd last seen him. And in all the right places.

"Second's nothing to complain about."

"It's nothing to brag about either," she pointed out, tearing her eyes away from his broad chest and trying to focus on the horse in front of her. She went back to brushing Beast, feeling slightly uncomfortable at the way Chris continued to silently watch her, as if he wanted to say something but wasn't sure how to bring it up. She finally turned and faced him. "What?"

He grabbed the front of his straw cowboy hat with his palm and adjusted it nervously. "Are you going to the dance tonight?"

Alicia felt a sizzle begin in her stomach and spiral outward. She fumbled with the brush, nearly dropping it and prayed she'd misheard him. Like his sister, Chris had a heart of gold and would do anything for his friends but, unlike Sydney, he was a flirt. A player. The type of guy with a new girl on his arm at every rodeo and never serious about any of them. He always had been and, she suspected, always would be. But, in spite of the way she and Sydney teased him about his philandering ways unmercifully growing up, she'd always harbored a huge crush on him, even if he'd never seen her as anything more than another pesky sister.

She stared at Beast's back, her hands no longer moving, unsure how to answer him. Chris must have seen her discomfort—he'd always been able to read her too well—and pushed himself away from the trailer, curling his lip with distaste.

"It's not for me," he exclaimed. "That'd be so wrong." He reached over and pinched her ribs, causing her to squeal and scoot away from his fingers. "It's for...someone else."

Alicia forced out a shaky laugh. "Are we back in high school again? Did some guy send you over here to see if I *like* him?" She tossed the brush into the bucket in the tack compartment and slipped a flake of alfalfa into a hay net before hanging it on the side of the trailer for both of her geldings, grateful they were easygoing enough to share. She arched a brow and cocked her hip to the side. "If some guy wants me to go to the dance with him tonight, he better be brave enough to ask me himself."

Chris ran his hand over her gelding's neck and shook his head, laughing. "Damn, woman, no wonder you're still single. You're brutal on us guys." He slapped her butt as he walked by. "Maybe I'll see you there tonight."

"Hey," she yelled after him. "That's mine, and unless you put a ring on this finger, keep your hands to yourself."

Chris shot her a quick wave but continued to laugh. She watched as he walked away, trying to drag her eyes away from admiring the way he filled out his jeans and to slow her racing heart. Then he looped his arm around the shoulders of a pretty redhead who didn't look like she'd ever touched a horse, let alone ridden one. *She might be looking for something to ride, but it isn't a horse.*

She rolled her eyes as she turned back to her animals, trying to quell the flutter in her stomach. She couldn't believe Chris could still make her feel this way. It didn't even make sense. She would never act on her feelings for him. In fact, she'd never told anyone, not even Sydney. It was just a stupid, girlish crush. Chris was nothing more than a friend, not to mention one of the most eligible cowboys on the circuit. And she was just a girl from the poor side of the barn who never registered as anything more than a nuisance on his radar.

CHRIS SAT ASTRIDE his bay gelding, Jaeger, in the practice arena, one leg casually looped around his saddle horn, while he and David waited for their turn. There were at least thirty pairs of team ropers in the slack and, so far, it was taking forever to get through them. At this rate, they were never going to make it in time for the barbecue tonight. His stomach rumbled, reminding him he hadn't eaten all day.

"Who was the girl you were talking to earlier?"

He casually glanced at his partner, David Greenly. He raised his brows at his friend. "Why? Interested?"

David shot him a disdainful glare. "Hardly."

They'd been rodeoing together for the last five years and when David encouraged him to go pro, Chris jumped at the chance. The two of them shared a common goal—to win the National Finals so they could open a roping school together. However, it took time to build their reputation and Chris wasn't known for his patience. He needed to remember they were taking it one step at a time, one go-round at a time. In the meantime, he wanted to enjoy every spare moment, while David seemed content to be a workaholic.

At this point, they knew each other well enough to finish the other's sentences. If he didn't watch himself, David would realize Chris was setting him up. Chris was tired of watching David push himself day after day, striving to be the best without any thought to what he was giving up. If he heard it once, he'd heard David complain about wanting to settle down and have kids a thousand times. Neither was high on Chris's list of priorities, but that didn't mean he couldn't help his friend have what he wanted—the family he'd missed growing up with a single dad on the rodeo circuit. Besides, he was tired of David being his wingman and never having a woman of his own. It was beginning to make him feel guilty, like he was hoarding the ladies all for himself.

Not that Chris had any intention of getting tied down like his sister had, regardless of his mother's begging for another grandchild. It wasn't that he had anything against the institution of marriage, he was just having too much fun enjoying his freedom.

He shot David a sly look. "I've talked to a lot of girls today. Which one are you talking about?"

"At the trailer. The barrel racer with the paint?" David absent-mindedly slapped the end of his rope against his thigh while his horse hung his head, bored and dozing. "She didn't look like one of your usual bunnies."

He was known to flirt with the women who lurked behind the chutes trying to find a cowboy to tame. Chris chuckled at the thought. Like he would ever be tamed. "Dark hair? Really pretty?"

"Yeah, she was pretty." David shrugged but didn't look away. "I suppose."

Chris could see he was interested but didn't want to appear overly so and laughed at him. "That's Alicia Kanani, Sydney's best friend. You don't remember her?"

He looked surprised. "The one who was rodeo queen a few years ago?"

"That's the one. Why? Want me to talk to her for you?"

David frowned and shook his head. "The last thing I need right now is a female distraction. You don't either," he pointed out. "Get your head in the game. We are sitting fourth in the standings and we need to be higher before the National Finals."

"Yes, sir." Chris snapped him a mock salute while David glared at him. "But if you think I'm going to act like a monk because you do, you're insane. With all these available females just vying for my attention? I mean, just look at them."

Chris nodded his head toward the fence where several women in miniskirts, cowboy boots, and half-shirts waved, trying to catch his attention. He winked at one of the women along the fence line and laughed as she started whispering to her friend. "You see? I'm just being friendly, the way my mama taught me."

"Sure you are." David shook his head and jerked his chin toward the chutes. "Quit fraternizing with the bunnies and pay attention. We're almost up."

The pair jogged their geldings to the gate and waited for their turn. As the steer was loaded into the chute, David walked his mount into the heeler box while Chris urged his into the opposite side and waited for the cowboy manning it to stretch the barrier rope across the front. He backed his horse into the corner of the box, feeling his haunches bunch under him, twitching with anticipation.

Chris settled the loop of his rope in his right hand, slipping his reins through his left until they were exactly the way he liked them. His gelding pawed his front foot, anticipating his opportunity to bolt forward. He inhaled deeply, practically tasting the damp earth. A slow smile spread over his lips. He loved this life.

Settling into the saddle, murmuring to his gelding, he let out the breath. He glanced over the chute at David and, seeing he was ready, nodded to the cowboy who released the steer from the chute. He nudged the gelding's sides, breaking from the box as the rope snapped, clearing him to make a clean run.

Swinging the loop over his head, he felt the rope slide deftly through his fingers until instinct told him it was exactly the size and position he wanted it to be. Reaching his arm forward, he tossed it perfectly over the steer's horns, flipping his hand over and catching the rope in his fingers as he simultaneously wound it around the saddle horn and turned his gelding. He directed the steer forward, the rope pressing against his thigh, as David aimed his loop downward to catch the steer's back feet. Watching over his shoulder, he heard the zip of the rope and saw David catch both feet. Chris spun his horse to face his partner, stretching their ropes taut as the official snapped his flag, signaling their time. 5.2. It was a great time; enough for first place, but they wouldn't know if they could hold their position until after tomorrow's performance.

The men rode toward one another causing the rope to loosen and slip from the steer's hind legs. David wound his rope as Chris followed the steer to the end of the arena where another cowboy removed his rope and a third opened the back gate for him to exit.

"Nice run, Chris."

He twisted in his saddle in time to see Alicia loading her horses into her trailer. "Thanks. You're leaving?" A curl of disappointment twisted through his gut, surprising him.

"Yeah, if I leave now, I can get home in time to help Dad feed the horses."

"Oh." He noticed David riding up behind him. "Hey, do you remember David Greenly?"

"Who wouldn't? You're practically rodeo royalty," she said, her pretty almond eyes turned toward David as she smiled up at him. "That was a great catch."

"Thanks," he muttered.

Chris looked from one to the other and frowned. David might be a man of few words but he'd never known him to be shy. He wondered at David's uncharacteristic surly frown. From the way his eyes slid over her curves, he was obviously attracted to her but you sure couldn't tell it by the look on his face. If he could get David to loosen up and find a nice woman to put up with his hyper-competitive, driven nature, they could start having fun roping again. Right now, David seemed intent on making it work.

He knew David's dad was putting him under a lot of pressure to make the Finals this year, and Chris could see it taking a toll. David needed to find a woman to loosen himself up while keeping his eyes on the championship, and Chris was sure Alicia was perfect for him. Sweet and fun, she'd always been a smart girl with ambition and a knack for talking them both out of trouble. She was just as driven as either of them. To tell the truth, growing up he'd always wanted to hook up with her himself but didn't want the complication that would arise from dating his sister's best friend. If David let himself, Chris knew he would fall for her dark beauty immediately. That is, if he would quit frowning and actually talk to her.

Chris leaned on the horn of his saddle as Alicia locked the back gate of her trailer and leaned against it. "How is your dad? I haven't seen him since the rodeo last year."

"Good, still working at the Diamond Bar." She crossed her arms, leaning against her trailer and smiled up at him.

"He hasn't moved on yet?"

Alicia cocked her head. "As if he would ever leave. He's been working for them since before I was born."

"And your mom?"

Alicia glanced at David, sitting stick-straight in the saddle, his eyes sliding over her as if he was trying to gauge her worth. It wasn't hard to see he was uncomfortable and wanted to move on. Chris knew David was irritated with him, but Alicia was sure to think she was the cause and Chris wanted to warn him to dial back the attitude. Just because his family was rodeo champion stock didn't mean Alicia was going to let someone treat her like chopped liver.

"She's still working for them too, running their house. I'm sure she'd love for you to stop by to say hi before you head out of town."

"I'm sure we could do that." Chris sat up and glanced at David. "Matter of fact, we're finished. If you want to wait for us, we can load our rig and head over to the house to help your dad feed." He didn't wait for David to agree, avoiding the pointed look he shot at Chris.

David sighed and shook his head, clenching his jaw. He refrained from commenting but it didn't hide his irritation. Chris glared at him in warning. What did David have to complain about? Chris was setting him up with a beautiful woman—unless David didn't realize what Chris was doing and thought Chris was trying to hook up with her. The thought almost made him laugh out loud. David would know by now that Chris liked women without strings attached. No commitments, ever. Alicia was the opposite. She was the girl you built forever with and Chris had no interest in forever. But, David? He was a different story.

Chris wasn't worried that Alicia might not be interested in his partner. He was the type of guy every girl wanted to settle down with—sturdy, dependable, ambitious—and for some reason, women were drawn to his "Aw shucks" demeanor. Chris had enough of them ask him about his friend to know the air of dependable, quiet strength surrounding him was what women sought in marriage material. They weren't looking for a fun-loving, irresponsible husband. They wanted a guy they could count on and, of the two of them, that was definitely David.

Alicia glanced at David again cautiously. "I'm sure Mama and Daddy would love for you guys to come have dinner with us but I'm not sure David wants to."

Chris shot David a warning look and cocked his head, smiling at Alicia's forthright comment. "Who cares what this guy wants." Chris jerked a thumb at David. "I'd love a home cooked meal. I'm sick of his ironed grilled cheese and cold French fries." He grimaced and she laughed.

"It can't be that bad."

"It is," David agreed, barely cracking a smile. Chris wished his friend would just lighten up for a few minutes. "I guess I'll get started loading the horses then. Sounds like I'll see you in just a bit, Alicia." David spun the horse and headed past several large stock trailers on his way to the one he shared with Chris.

Alicia watched him leave, curiously, before raising her brows and turning to Chris. "Wow, he's kinda intense."

Chris stifled a chuckle, glad she wasn't judging him by their first encounter. "Yeah, but he's a good guy and I know he's got my back no matter what."

"You mean he'd bail you out of any kind of trouble you get yourself into," she said, jingling her keys, trying to hide the smile tugging at the corners of her lips.

"I mean, he has. Several times," he clarified before giving her a guilty smile. "Probably will again before this weekend is over." Chris glanced back in the direction David had gone. "I better go help him. If you want to head out, we'll just be a few minutes behind you. I think, after all these years, I can still remember the way," he said before winking at her and watching her pull out of the arena before nudging his gelding toward his trailer.

As he rode closer, he could see the fury in David's face and wondered at the wisdom of their dinner plans.

"What the hell was that?" David tossed the saddle blanket into the trailer. "I thought we were going to go to the barbecue before we headed out tonight. We were leaving, remember?"

Chris shrugged off his friend's anger. "So? We have a change in plans. It's not a big deal." He loosened his gelding's cinch. "Since when do you complain about a meal you don't have to pay for?"

"I'm not complaining about the meal. I'm complaining about you being so obvious." He leaned over his gelding's back and crossed his wrists. "If I want a date, I'll get one myself. I don't need your help."

"Yeah, because it's happened so often over the past three months."

David shook his head and sighed as he brushed the horse. "Have you ever stopped to think that not everyone is like you? You have more notches on your bed than I have trophy buckles."

Chris laughed out loud. He wasn't offended by David's comment. He knew he had the reputation of being a playboy and he'd never tried to correct the rumors that he slept with the women he flirted with. He'd assumed they would get cleared up eventually. The truth was, when they were on the road, he gave most women a ride home only when they were too drunk to drive, and then he slept in his truck or a spare bedroom if they were generous. He'd seen the devastation drunk driving created after losing a friend on her way home from a rodeo. After that night, he vowed to do his best to see any woman home safely. He'd never thought it might make him look like a dog.

Then there were the women he took home because he was afraid if they were left to their own devices, they'd be taken advantage of by some of the less than gentlemanly cowboys who preyed on "buckle bunnies." Sure, he was a red-blooded man and there were nights he didn't go to bed alone, but not nearly as many as people suspected. But only Sydney knew the truth. These rumors following him were getting out of hand and he was going to need to clear all of it up before it bit him in the ass.

"Walk a mile in these boots, my friend, and you might find it's not all you think it is." He shook his head. "I'm sick of listening to women trying figure out how to get your attention. Alicia is a pretty, sweet woman who can cowboy with the best of them. I just thought you two have a lot in common and you're not the type of guy to love 'em and leave 'em so I know you won't hurt her. Besides, you'd better settle down and start having that family you talk about soon or you're gonna be too old to have kids."

"Whatever, Chris." David rolled his eyes and tossed the brush into the shelf on the door. "You've already roped me into this. It's not like I can back out now. It just would've been nice to have some warning."

"It's feeding some horses. We have to do the same with our own."

David untied his horse's lead rope and loaded him into the trailer. "Just do me a favor and ask first next time."

"Sure." Chris chuckled quietly, congratulating himself on a match well-made. Tonight they'd have dinner and, hopefully, he'd convince the pair to go to the dance. Tomorrow, they'd head out and, if all went according to plan, David would be so busy watching for Alicia at the next rodeo that Chris might get ten minutes all to himself.

Chapter Two

ALICIA PULLED THE truck into the circular drive, hoping there was enough room for both rigs to fit in front of her parents' tiny modular home. She was worried about Chris and David coming over. She wasn't blind. She knew Chris was trying to set her up with David, which was embarrassing enough, but she didn't really want him to see where she lived. Her parents worked hard but she wasn't exactly proud of the fact her mother was a glorified housekeeper and her father cleaned stalls for a living. She sighed, guilt sweeping over her. She hated feeling ashamed of her upbringing but the emotions wouldn't stay buried.

Face it, you're poor, she scolded herself. *That's not going to change anytime soon.*

She'd always been the poor kid growing up. When she was young, she'd worn clothes that smelled like mothballs and musty books, never owning anything new or firsthand. What she wouldn't have given for a trip to the mall, just once. Even when they'd moved into West Hills and she'd gone to high school, everything had been second hand. She'd been grateful for even the little she had, but it wasn't easy when she saw girls coming to school in every new fad, while she was wearing the same jeans she'd had for four years. She hadn't wanted anyone to know, so she learned to sew, managing to refurbish thrift store deals into Western couture, and made all of her own riding shirts for rodeos. She'd even sold a few of her designs to other queen contestants to make ends meet and help her parents out. Chris knew because he'd seen it firsthand over the many years she and Sydney had been friends, but what would David Greenly think when he saw what little they had?

You saw the look on his face. He'll think you're not worth his time.

She sighed as her mother came onto the porch. Alicia had already called her from the rodeo grounds to let her know Chris and David were coming to dinner. Of course, her mother was thrilled. Both of her parents adored Chris since meeting him. Who could blame them? Everyone loved Chris. He was one of those people who excelled at everything with minimal effort. His easygoing nature drew others to him like a magnet and he never seemed to lack people vying for his attention, especially women. Not that he ever turned them away. In all the years she'd known him, she couldn't believe he'd never realized she had a crush on him, too. Maybe, like David, he didn't think she was worth his time and attention.

Alicia unloaded her horses and turned them loose into the small pasture beside their home. Both geldings took off at a run, kicking their hooves into the air as she hung the halters on the hook beside the gate.

"Where's Dad?" she called to her mother.

"He's out in the mare barn, feeding." Her mother looked toward the gate. "Where are Chris and his friend?"

"They're loading up and will be here in a few minutes. Does Dad need my help?"

Her mother waved her off. "The boys can help him. I'm going to head over to the house and get dinner on the table for Mrs. Langdon. I'll be back in a few minutes but can you take the lasagna out and put the garlic bread into the oven in ten minutes?"

"Sure, Mom." Alicia headed into the house, plugging her phone into the charger on the counter. "Anything else you need me to do?" She took a bottle of water from the refrigerator.

"Nope, Dad will be in after he checks on the yearlings."

Alicia sighed as she watched her mother walk down the pathway leading to the main house. She'd been the Langdons' housekeeper and cook throughout her pregnancy while Alicia's father ran the entire stable of champion cutting horses. For years, the Langdon family had been trying to get Alicia to work for them, showing their horses and training, but she couldn't give up on rodeo and settle for the same life her parents had. The Langdons were wonderful people who had taken care of both of her parents over the many years in their employ but Alicia

refused to quit rodeo until she reached the pinnacle—
the National Finals Rodeo. She had to prove to herself
and everyone else that she wasn't just some poor kid the
Langdons helped. Reaching her goal would also help her
do the one thing she wanted most: help her father train
his own horses instead of someone else's. Watching her
mother head over to the Langdons when she should be
having dinner with her family made Alicia realize that
nothing short of the Finals would be enough.

She sighed, rising from the chair as the buzzer
sounded, and reached for the oven mitts her mother
left on the counter. This year she was closer than ever to
making the Finals. She might not win every rodeo but the
second place purses were adding up. If her luck and her
geldings continued to hold out, she'd place in the top ten
this season and be in Las Vegas competing this Decem-
ber. The mere thought caused flutters of nervousness in
her stomach.

Her parents didn't have any idea what she was planning but she already had her eyes on a ranch on the
outskirts of town. Nothing as large as the property
the Langdons owned, but it was plenty of room for the
three of them to build a house and enough space for her
father to finally raise his own horses, the way he'd always
talked about doing. Adding this season's winnings to
what she'd already saved over the past two years should
give her enough for a nice down payment. But she didn't
want to get her parents' hopes up until she put an offer
on the place. She couldn't bear to get their hopes up only
to have it fall apart later.

DAVID PARKED THE truck behind Alicia's trailer and looked around at the tiny house. "Not much to the place, huh?"

"We can't all have parents who own cattle ranches or were world champions," Chris pointed out, wondering if David realized he sounded like a snob.

His friend arched a brow at him in indignation. "I wasn't criticizing, just stating a fact. Sensitive much?" David climbed from the driver's seat and Chris followed.

Maybe he was being a bit oversensitive but he knew how Alicia hated being judged for her parents' lack of money and he didn't want to see David get off on the wrong foot from the start. Noah Kanani had come from Hawaii and worked hard to earn the respect of Bradley Langdon, one of the largest cutting horse breeders in the nation. Jessenia was one of the sweetest women he'd ever known and he'd thought of her like a second mother when he was younger. As much as he hated to see how hard she worked as both housekeeper and cook for the Langdon family, he could only imagine how it troubled Alicia.

"Hey," Alicia called from the front porch. "You can either tie your horses to the trailer or turn them out in the pasture behind the house. We don't have any broodmares out there right now."

David glanced at Chris, letting him make the decision. "Pasture?"

"Might as well. You want me to do it and you can head inside?" Chris wagged his brows at his friend suggestively.

"Why don't I handle the horses?" David muttered, opening the back of the trailer.

"Chicken," Chris chuckled and shrugged. "Whatever. More food for me." He hurried up the porch steps and followed Alicia into the house, immediately hit with a whiff of Italian spices and garlic. His stomach rumbled loudly and Alicia glanced at him over her shoulder, laughing.

"Dinner is just about ready, if you want to wash up in the bathroom at the end of the hall. Towels are in the bottom cabinet."

"I remember," he said, winking at her. "David should be in shortly. Does your dad need any help?"

She bent over and checked the bread in the oven. "No, Mom just left for the main house but she'll be right back." She shot him a sideways glance and the corner of his mouth curved up. "I think she's pretty excited to see you."

"I've missed your mom. I know I should stop by more often when I'm home. But you know how it is." He shrugged by way of apology. "I'm on the road most of the time and when I do come back, Dad needs my help at the ranch. Time flies and I never realize it's gone."

"I know."

Chris narrowed his eyes, wondering if she really did know. She'd never travelled as much as he and David did, staying close to her parents and helping them whenever she could. Even at that, she was still sitting pretty in the standings.

He watched her adjust the tray of bread in the oven, trying not to notice the rounded curve of her rear, although parts of him were making the task extremely difficult. She'd always been a pretty girl but she was his sister's skinny best friend, smart enough to be a year ahead of him in school even though they were the same age. Back in high school he'd almost asked her to the prom but hadn't been brave enough. When she told him she was going to a rodeo instead, he insisted on driving her and was there to celebrate her first professional win. In the end, he never did ask her out, for fear of jeopardizing their friendship. Instead, he'd forced himself to back off, admiring Alicia from a distance. He arched a brow. He didn't remember her having these curves back then, or even at his sister's wedding.

The front door slammed and Chris tore his gaze, and wandering thoughts, from Alicia's backside, poking his head around the corner to see Jessenia come inside.

"Cristobel!" She hurried forward and enveloped him in a hug, squeezing him impressively for such a tiny woman.

"Jessie!" He laughed at the Spanish nickname she'd given him in high school, as he lifted her from the ground and swung her around once. He placed her back on the floor. "I'm sorry I haven't been by sooner."

She gave him a frown. "I should hope so. I don't even know how long it's been since I've seen you," she scolded in her thick Spanish accent.

Chris tried to look sheepish when he heard the clomping of boots on the steps of the front porch. The door opened as Noah came inside, making sure not to track dirt into Jessie's immaculate house. "I sure hope that cowboy putting horses in the back is with you, young man."

Chris laughed and thrust out a hand to Alicia's father. "He's my roping partner. It's good to see you again, sir."

"Alicia, why don't you go see if that young man outside needs anything else?" Jessie suggested.

Chris wondered if she wasn't already having the same thoughts as he was about the pair and looked over at Alicia, leaning against the side of the doorway, watching their interaction.

"Sure, Mom." Alicia pushed away from the wall, rolling her eyes as she moved past them to head outside.

"Don't mind her," Noah said as she closed the door. "She's just mad about quitting rodeo."

"I CAN'T BELIEVE I let him get me involved in this," David muttered as he threw two flakes of hay to the geldings.

It wasn't as if they didn't have plenty they needed to work on. What they really should have done was head to Chris's parents' ranch to practice before their second go-round tomorrow. If they didn't get some better times, there was no way they were going to stay in the top ten and get to Vegas. It pissed him off that Chris would rather spend precious practice time flirting with girls from his past, and trying to get him to do the same.

"You know, some people think talking to your horse is a sign of insanity."

The quiet laughter at the pasture gate made him clench his jaw. She might be a great girl but he wasn't looking to get involved with anyone nor did he have time for a relationship, contrary to what Chris seemed to think.

"Yeah, well, that tends to happen anyway when Chris Thomas is your roping partner."

She leaned her arms over the fence, resting her chin on them. "He does have that effect on people," she laughed. "Need some help?" She pushed herself from the fence and opened the gate.

"I'm about finished, unless you want to grab a can of grain from the trailer?"

"Sure," she said, hurrying toward their trailer in front of the house.

David couldn't help but notice the way her full lips curved into a pretty smile making her dark eyes light up or the slight sway of her hips as she left. She was exactly the type of girl he was attracted to, a girl-next-door with natural beauty, even with her hair pulled back and no makeup. Chris knew it, too, damn him. But what he didn't realize was that it only made him more driven to focus on winning so he could earn enough money to be able to settle down and have the things he wanted in his future—a wife, kids, his own ranch—like his brother.

She returned with a coffee can of grain, shaking it. The horses jerked their heads up and whinnied their approval as she came near, drawing him out of his pointless daydreams, and she passed it to him over the fence.

"Nice looking boys," she commented, jerking her chin toward the animals. "You two are doing pretty well in the standings, at least for now."

David shrugged. "Not if I can't keep Chris's head in the game."

She gave him an understanding smile. "You guys have been roping together for almost five years, right? You know he'll manage to pull it out in the end. I have no idea how he always seems to do it but he does. I wish I had that talent."

He caught her frown from the corner of his eye as he poured the grain over the flakes of hay and locked the pasture gate. "Let's hope so," David grumbled. "Personally, I'm tired of almost making it to the Finals. I want to be there this year and I'm not letting him lose focus."

She cocked her head at him, as if she was trying to read his thoughts, and he wondered if he'd said more than he should've. He didn't normally let his mouth get ahead of his brain and good sense but for some reason this woman had him acting out of character, admitting things he wouldn't under normal circumstances.

"I mean…" He closed his mouth, wishing he'd just kept it shut from the beginning, and wondered again how she was able to get him to let his guard down so quickly.

"I know what you mean," she cut him off. "It's hard to come so close over and over only to be disappointed, especially when it's not your fault." She glanced up at the back of the house. "I'm hoping to make it to Vegas, too. Even if other people do have a different opinion as to where I should be."

He stopped walking and stared at her, knowing there was far more she wasn't saying. He arched a brow. "Maybe we have more in common than either of us thought."

She smiled at him, and the sadness he'd seen in her eyes disappeared for a moment. "Maybe we do," she agreed.

"So, tell me," he began, looking around him at the various fenced pastures. "What's up with this place?"

"Dad's run the day-to-day operations for the Diamond Bar for the last twenty-five years and Mom works for them in the house. I guess you could say it's turned into a family affair." The frown was back, marring her brow. "They're nice people and they've been good to us."

"You're sure it's fine for the boys to be in the pasture?"

"What?" She glanced at the horses quietly eating. "Oh, they're fine. It's not like you guys are staying long. It's just dinner."

David felt a twinge of disappointment. She was different than he'd expected her to be. He'd assumed any woman Chris introduced him to would be shallow and, well, a floozy. Alicia wasn't like that at all. He found himself interested in her and wanted to spend more time with her. He needed to stay focused, and keep Chris focused, but they obviously weren't going to do any practicing tonight. Why not invite this pretty barrel racer to the dance tonight after all? If they weren't going to work, maybe one night of fun with an attractive woman wouldn't be such a horrible idea. If nothing else, it might get Chris to quit pestering him.

"THE PLACE LOOKS great, Jessie. I like the new counters in the kitchen," Chris said, reaching for another piece of garlic bread, wiping the excess butter from his hands on the paper towel beside his plate. "Did you have it professionally done?"

"No, I did it myself." Alicia shook her head as her mother blushed slightly at his compliment, "But, thank you."

Alicia caught Chris's eye. "I think you have a little something right there." She rubbed at the end of her nose. David choked back a laugh, covering his mouth with his napkin. Even her father laughed at the joke.

"You hush," her mother warned, playfully slapping at Alicia's arm with her fingertips. "He can compliment my taste any time he wants to if it means he'll come around more often."

Chris smirked at Alicia and turned toward her father. "Dad told me Bradley just sold one of his studs for $12,000. Was it the one you've been training?"

"He was a great horse before I ever got my hands on him. I was just lucky to work with such a talented stud."

Alicia watched her father shake his head, lowering his eyes in humility. She hated that he wouldn't take any credit for the work he did. He was an amazing trainer and was wasting time mucking stalls and grooming for someone else. He should be training and selling his own horses for that price. If only she was able to get the down payment for that property sooner… She looked down at her plate, suddenly losing her appetite.

"That's pretty impressive, Noah," Chris commented. "You still afraid of them, Jessie?"

Her mother laughed quietly. "Not afraid, just cautious. They're so big! Did Alicia tell you she will probably be working with Noah soon?"

"Really?" David asked as both cowboys turned to Alicia in surprise. He'd been quiet throughout the meal and Alicia glanced up at him.

She set her napkin on the table and cleared her throat, unsure how to answer the question. She had no intention of taking Bradley Langdon up on his offer to train and show his horses. She wasn't about to get trapped into the same life her parents had, working for a dream that wasn't her own, but she hadn't broken her decision to her parents yet. Until she could offer an alternative solution, or purchase the property she wanted, she'd been stalling.

"Her riding prowess hasn't gone unnoticed all these years and Bradley wants her to show his horses. Maybe even start training a few and giving lessons."

"That's a big accomplishment," David acknowledged, smiling at her.

Her father looked at her proudly and her heart ached. He saw it as such a compliment and she saw it as a prison sentence. How could she ever make him understand?

"I guess," she agreed, hoping they would assume her hesitancy was discomfort and change the subject. "I still have to finish out this rodeo season," she pointed out.

Why was it that no one seemed to care that she wanted nothing to do with helping anyone else earn money from her work? If she ever quit rodeo to train, it was going to be to train her own barrel horses and give lessons on her own ranch. Why did everyone assume she would jump at the chance to train for the Diamond Bar.

Chris frowned, his brows dipping low. "I think it's a waste of talent." Every set of eyes at the table spun to look at him. "I mean, Alicia is an amazing barrel racer, she always has been. Why quit to train cutting horses? Do you even *want* to show cutting horses?"

She glanced at her father, biting her lower lip nervously. He turned to her expectantly, waiting for her answer. She couldn't help but appreciate that Chris seemed to understand her desire to race, voicing her thoughts, but she could've kicked him when she saw the disappointment in her father's eyes. "I don't know. I never really thought about it before."

Chris sighed and rolled his eyes. "You've always talked about being a barrel racer and teaching other girls to run. I never once heard you say anything about showing." He wiped his mouth with his napkin and placed it in his plate. "In fact, I remember you laughing at the girls who went to horse shows."

She saw David's body jerk to the side and Chris shot a glare at David. Alicia silently thanked him for shutting Chris up, even if it was with a kick under the table. This was something she needed to talk about with her parents privately. She didn't need his help or, in this case, him instigating trouble.

CHRIS RUBBED AT the knot forming on his shin and glowered at David.

"Are you guys ready for dessert? Blackberry pie?" Jessie asked, looking at him pointedly. "If I remember right, that's your favorite, isn't it, Cristobel?"

He gave her a grin. "I love your blackberry pie but you've stuffed me with lasagna and garlic bread." He shot a sly look at David who was watching Alicia intently. "I guess I could have a small piece and then work it off dancing tonight."

"I thought you said you wanted to head out?" Chris didn't miss David's suspicious glance.

"We should go to the dance and have some fun." He nodded toward Alicia across the table. "I know how much this one likes to dance. Maybe she could teach you a thing or two. Your moves are pretty horrendous."

"I don't know," Alicia hemmed. "I have to be back down there early tomorrow for the next go-round." She stood and started to clear the table.

"You'll do fine, hon," Noah chuckled. "Beast knows the pattern in his sleep."

Alicia rolled her eyes as she hurried to the sink with the plates, not wanting her father to see her irritation. She needed to focus on tomorrow's run. If she came in first it would move her up in the standings, bump her above Delilah, and add a hefty chunk to her savings. She had to be at the top of her game, not exhausted from dancing with a couple of cowboys, no matter how ruggedly good looking they might be. Although, an ice cold beer and some loud music might curb the frustration building in her right now.

"Come on, Ali." Chris came up behind her with a stack of plates. "It'll be like old times." He cocked his head to the side and gave her the puppy dog eyes that used to get him his way with his sister.

She glanced up at David, who followed Chris into the kitchen, bearing more dishes. He shrugged and looked resigned to Chris getting his way again. She wanted to be angry and shake him. Maybe if people told him no once in a while, he'd understand responsibility and that life wasn't all about fun.

Instead, she looked back at his pleading blue eyes and sighed. Her heart thumped in her chest as he took a step closer before lowering his voice.

"Come on, Ali. You know you want to go."

She did and couldn't fight it when her heart did a flip in her chest. Alicia sighed. "Fine." How did he always manage to turn her brains to mush?

About the Author
_____

T. J. KLINE was bitten by the horse bug early and began training horses at fourteen as well as competing in rodeos and winning several rodeo queen competitions but has always known writing was her first love. She also writes under the name Tina Klinesmith. In her spare time, she can be found spending as much time as possible laughing hysterically with her husband, teens, and their menagerie of pets in Northern California.

Discover great authors, exclusive offers, and more at hc.com.

Give in to your impulses . . .
Read on for a sneak peek at seven brand-new
e-book original tales of romance
from HarperCollins.
Available now wherever e-books are sold.

VARIOUS STATES OF UNDRESS: GEORGIA

By Laura Simcox

MAKE IT LAST

A BOWLER UNIVERSITY NOVEL

By Megan Erickson

HERO BY NIGHT

BOOK THREE: INDEPENDENCE FALLS

By Sara Jane Stone

MAYHEM

By Jamie Shaw

SINFUL REWARDS 1
A BILLIONAIRES AND BIKERS NOVELLA
By Cynthia Sax

FORBIDDEN
AN UNDER THE SKIN NOVEL
By Charlotte Stein

HER HIGHLAND FLING
A NOVELLA
By Jennifer McQuiston

An Excerpt from

VARIOUS STATES OF UNDRESS: GEORGIA

by Laura Simcox

Laura Simcox concludes her fun, flirty
Various States of Undress series with a
presidential daughter, a hot baseball player,
and a tale of love at the ballgame.

An Excerpt from

VARIOUS STATES OF UNDRESS: GEORGIA

by Laura Simcox

Laura Simcox concludes her fun, flirty
Various States of Undress series with a
presidential daughter, a hot baseball player,

"**U**h. Hi."

Georgia splayed her hand over the front of her wet blouse and stared. The impossibly tanned guy standing just inside the doorway—wearing a tight T-shirt, jeans, and a smile— was as still as a statue. A statue with fathomless, unblinking chocolate brown eyes. She let her gaze drop from his face to his broad chest. "Oh. Hello. I was expecting someone else."

He didn't comment, but when she lifted her gaze again, past his wide shoulders and carved chin, she watched his smile turn into a grin, revealing way-too-sexy brackets at the corners of his mouth. He walked down the steps and onto the platform where she stood. He had to be at least 6'3", and testosterone poured off him like heat waves on the field below. She shouldn't stare at him, right? Damn. Her gaze flicked from him to the glass wall but moved right back again.

"Scared of heights?" he asked. His voice was a slow, deep Southern drawl. Sexy deep. "Maybe you oughta sit down."

"No, thanks. I was just . . . looking for something."

Looking for something? Like what—a tryst with a stranger in the press box? Her face heated, and she clutched the water bottle, the plastic making a snapping sound under her fingers. "So . . . how did you get past my agents?"

He smiled again. "They know who I am."

"And you are?"

"Brett Knox."

His name sounded familiar. "Okay. I'm Georgia Fulton. It's nice to meet you," she said, putting down her water.

He shook her hand briefly. "You, too. But I just came up here to let you know that I'm declining the interview. Too busy."

Georgia felt herself nodding in agreement, even as she realized *exactly* who Brett Knox was. He was the star catcher—and right in front of her, shooting her down before she'd even had a chance to ask. Such a typical jock.

"I'm busy, too, which is why I'd like to set up a time that's convenient for both of us," she said, even though she hoped it wouldn't be necessary. But she couldn't very well walk into the news station without accomplishing what she'd been tasked with—pinning him down. Georgia was a team player. So was Brett, literally.

"I don't want to disappoint my boss, and I'm betting you feel the same way about yours," she continued.

"Sure. I sign autographs, pose for photos, visit Little League teams. Like I said, I'm busy."

"That's nice." She nodded. "I'm flattered that you found the time to come all the way up to the press box and tell me, in person, that you don't have time for an interview. Thanks."

He smiled a little. "You're welcome." Then he stretched, his broad chest expanding with the movement. He flexed his long fingers, braced a hand high on the post, and grinned at her again. Her heart flipped down into her stomach. Oh, no.

"I get it, you know. I've posed for photos and signed autographs, too. I've visited hospitals and ribbon cutting ceremonies, and I know it makes people happy. But public appearances can be draining, and it takes time away from work. Right?"

"Right." He gave her a curious look. "We have that in common, though it's not exactly the same. I may be semifamous in Memphis, but I don't have paparazzi following me around, and I like it that way. You interviewing me would turn into a big hassle."

"I won't take much of your time. Just think of me as another reporter." She ventured a warm, inviting smile, and Brett's dark eyes widened. "The paparazzi don't follow me like they do my sisters. I'm the boring one."

"Really?" He folded his arms across his lean middle, and his gaze traveled slowly over her face.

She felt her heart speed up. "Yes, really."

"I beg to differ."

Before she could respond, he gave her another devastating smile and jogged up the steps. It was the best view she'd had all day. When Brett disappeared, she collapsed back against the post. He was right, of course. She wasn't just another reporter; she was the president's brainy daughter—who secretly lusted after athletes. And she'd just met a hell of an athlete.

Talk about a hot mess.

An Excerpt from

MAKE IT LAST
A Bowler University Novel
by Megan Erickson

The last installment in Megan Erickson's daringly
sexy Bowler University series finds Cam Ruiz
back in his hometown of Paradise, where he comes
face-to-face with the only girl he ever loved.

Cam sighed, feeling the weight of responsibility pressing down on his shoulders. But if he didn't help his mom, who would?

He jingled his keys in his pocket and turned to walk toward his truck. It was nice of Max and Lea to visit him on their road trip. College had been some of the best years of his life. Great friends, fun parties, hot girls.

But now it felt like a small blip, like a week vacation instead of three and a half years. And now he was right back where he started.

As he walked by the alley beside the restaurant, something flickered out of the corner of his eye.

He turned and spotted her legs first. One foot bent at the knee and braced on the brick wall, the other flat on the ground. Her head was bent, a curtain of hair blocking her face. But he knew those legs. He knew those hands. And he knew that hair, a light brown that held just a glint of strawberry in the sun. He knew by the end of August it'd be lighter and redder and she'd laugh about that time she put lemon juice in it. It'd backfired and turned her hair orange.

The light flickered again but it was something weird and artificial, not like the menthols she had smoked. Back when he knew her.

As she lowered her hand down to her side, he caught sight of the small white cylinder. It was an electronic cigarette. She'd quit.

She raised her head then, like she knew someone watched her, and he wanted to keep walking, avoid this awkward moment. Avoid those eyes he didn't think he'd ever see again and never thought he'd wanted to see again. But now that his eyes locked on her hazel eyes—the ones he knew began as green on the outside of her iris and darkened to brown by the time they met her pupil—he couldn't look away. His boots wouldn't move.

The small cigarette fell to the ground with a soft click and she straightened, both her feet on the ground.

And that was when he noticed the wedge shoes. And the black apron. What was she doing here?

"Camilo."

Other than his mom, she was the only one who used his full name. He'd heard her say it while laughing. He'd her moan it while he was inside her. He'd heard her sigh it with an eye roll when he made a bad joke. But he'd never heard it the way she said it now, with a little bit of fear and anxiety and . . . longing? He took a deep breath to steady his voice. "Tatum."

He hadn't spoken her name since that night Trevor called him and told him what she did. The night the future that he'd set out for himself and for her completely changed course.

She'd lost some weight in the four years since he'd last seen her. He'd always loved her curves. She had it all—thighs, ass and tits in abundance. Naked, she was a fucking vision.

Damn it, he wasn't going there.

But now her face looked thinner, her clothes hung a little loose and he didn't like this look as much. Not that she probably gave a fuck about his opinion anymore.

She still had her gorgeous hair, pinned up halfway with a bump in front, and a smattering of freckles across the bridge of her nose and on her cheekbones. And she still wore her makeup exactly the same—thickly mascaraed eyelashes, heavy eyeliner that stretched to a point on the outside of her eyes, like a modern-day Audrey Hepburn.

She was still beautiful. And she still took his breath away.

And his heart felt like it was breaking all over again.

And he hated her even more for that.

Her eyes were wide. "What are you doing here?"

Something in him bristled at that. Maybe it was because he didn't feel like he belonged here. But then, she didn't either. She never did. *They* never did.

But there was no longer a *they*.

An Excerpt from

HERO BY NIGHT
Book Three: Independence Falls
by Sara Jane Stone

Travel back to Independence Falls in Sara Jane
Stone's next thrilling read. Armed with a golden
retriever and a concealed weapons permit, Lena
Clark is fighting for normal. She served her
country, but the experience left her afraid to be
touched and estranged from her career-military
family. Staying in Independence Falls, and finding
a job, seems like the first step to reclaiming her life
and preparing for the upcoming medal ceremony—
until the town playboy stumbles into her bed . . .

Sometimes beauty knocked a man on his ass, leaving him damn near desperate for a taste, a touch, and hopefully a round or two between the sheets—or tied up in them. The knockout blonde with the large golden retriever at her feet took the word "beautiful" to a new level.

Chad Summers stared at her, unable to look away or dim the smile on his face. He usually masked his interest better, stopping short of looking like he was begging for it before learning a woman's name. But this mysterious beauty had special written all over her.

She stared at him, her gaze open and wanting. For a heartbeat. Then she turned away, her back to the party as she stared out at Eric Moore's pond.

Her hair flowed in long waves down her back. One look left him wishing he could wrap his hand around her shiny locks and pull. His gaze traveled over her back, taking in the outline of gentle curves beneath her flowing, and oh-so-feminine, floor-length dress. The thought of the beauty's long skirt decorating her waist propelled him into motion. Chad headed in her direction, moving away from the easy, quiet conversation about God-knew-what on the patio.

The blonde, a mysterious stranger in a sea of familiar faces, might be the spark this party needed. He was a few feet away when the dog abandoned his post at her side and cut Chad off. Either the golden retriever was protecting his owner, or the animal was in cahoots with the familiar voice calling his name.

"Chad Summers!"

The blonde turned at the sound, looking first at him, her blue eyes widening as if surprised at how close he stood, and then at her dog. From the other direction, a familiar face with short black hair—Susan maybe?—marched toward him.

Without a word, Maybe Susan stopped by his side and raised her glass. With a dog in front of him, trees to one side, and an angry woman on his other, there was no escape.

"Hi there." He left off her name just in case he'd guessed wrong, but offered a warm, inviting smile. Most women fell for that grin, but if Maybe Susan had at one time—and seeing her up close, she looked very familiar, though he could swear he'd never slept with her—she wasn't falling for it today.

She poured the cool beer over his head, her mouth set in a firm line. "That was for my sister. Susan Lewis? You spent the night with her six months ago and never called."

Chad nodded, silently grateful he hadn't addressed the pissed-off woman by her sister's name. "My apologies, ma'am."

"You're a dog," Susan's sister announced. The animal at his feet stepped forward as if affronted by the comparison.

"For the past six months, my little sister has talked about you, saving every article about your family's company," the angry woman continued.

Whoa . . . Yes, he'd taken Susan Lewis out once and they'd ended the night back at his place, but he could have sworn they were on the same page. Hell, he'd heard her say the words, *I'm not looking for anything serious*, and he'd believed her. It was one freaking night. He didn't think he needed signed documents that spelled out his intentions and hers.

"She's practically built a shrine to you," she added, waving her empty beer cup. "Susan was ready to plan your wedding."

"Again, I'm sorry, but it sounds like there was a miscommunication." Chad withdrew a bandana from his back pocket, one that had belonged to his father, and wiped his brow. "But wedding bells are not in my future. At least not anytime soon."

The angry sister shook her head, spun on her heels, and marched off.

Chad turned to the blonde and offered a grin. She looked curious, but not ready to run for the hills. "I guess I made one helluva first impression."

"Hmm." She glanced down at her dog as if seeking comfort in the fact that he stood between them.

"I'm Chad Summers." He held out his hand—the one part of his body not covered in beer.

"You're Katie's brother." She glanced briefly at his extended hand, but didn't take it.

He lowered his arm, still smiling. "Guilty."

"Lena." She nodded to the dog. "That's Hero."

"Nice to meet you both." He looked up the hill. Country music drifted down from the house. Someone had finally added some life to the party. Couples moved to the beat on the blue stone patio, laughing and drinking under the clear Oregon night sky. In the corner, Liam Trulane tossed logs into a fire pit.

"After I dry off," Chad said, turning back to the blonde, "how about a dance?"

"No."

An Excerpt from

MAYHEM

by Jamie Shaw

A straitlaced college freshman is drawn
to a sexy and charismatic rock star in this
fabulous debut New Adult novel for fans
of Jamie McGuire and Jay Crownover!

"I can't believe I let you talk me into this." I tug at the black hem of the stretchy nylon skirt my best friend squeezed me into, but unless I want to show the top of my panties instead of the skin of my thighs, there's nothing I can do. After casting yet another uneasy glance at the long line of people stretched behind me on the sidewalk, I shift my eyes back to the sun-warmed fabric pinched between my fingers and grumble, "The least you could've done was let me wear some leggings."

I look like Dee's closet drank too much and threw up on me. She somehow talked me into wearing this mini-skirt—which skintight doesn't even begin to describe—and a hot-pink top that shows more cleavage than should be legal. The front of it drapes all the way down to just above my navel, and the bottom exposes a pale sliver of skin between the hem of the shirt and the top of my skirt. The fabric matches my killer hot-pink heels.

Literally, killer. Because I know I'm going to fall on my face and die.

I'm fiddling with the skirt again when one of the guys near us in line leans in close, a jackass smile on his lips. "I think you look hot."

"I have a boyfriend," I counter, but Dee just scoffs at me.

"She means *thank you*," she shoots back, chastising me with her tone until the guy flashes us another arrogant smile—he's stuffed into an appallingly snug graphic-print tee that might as well say "douche bag" in its shiny metallic lettering, and even Dee can't help but make a face before we both turn away.

She and I are the first ones in line for the show tonight, standing by the doors to Mayhem under the red-orange glow of a setting summer sun. She's been looking forward to this night for weeks, but I was more excited about it before my boyfriend of three years had to back out.

"Brady is a jerk," she says, and all I can do is sigh because I wish those two could just get along. Deandra and I have been best friends since preschool, but Brady and I have been dating since my sophomore year of high school and living together for the past two months. "He should be here to appreciate how gorgeous you look tonight, but nooo, it's always work first with him."

"He moved all the way here to be with me, Dee. Cut him some slack, all right?"

She grumbles her frustration until she catches me touching my eyelids for the zillionth time tonight. Yanking my fingers away, she orders, "Stop messing with it. You'll smear."

I stare down at my shadowy fingertips and rub them together. "Tell me the truth," I say, flicking the clumped powder away. "Do I look like a clown?"

"You look smoking hot!" she assures me with a smile.

I finally feel like I'm beginning to loosen up when a guy walks right past us like he's going to cut in line. In dark shades and a baggy black knit cap that droops in the back, he flicks a cigarette to the ground, and my eyes narrow on him.

Dee and I have been waiting for way too long to let some self-entitled jerk cut in front of us, so when he knocks on the door to the club, I force myself to speak up.

"They're not letting people in yet," I say, hoping he takes the hint. Even with my skyscraper heels, I feel dwarfed standing next to him. He has to be at least six-foot-two, maybe taller.

He turns his head toward me and lowers his shades, smirking like something's funny. His wrist is covered with string bracelets and rubber bracelets and a thick leather cuff, and three of his fingernails on each hand are painted black. But his eyes are what steal the words from my lips—a greenish shade of light gray. They're stunning.

When the door opens, he turns back to it and locks hands with the bouncer.

"You're late," the bouncer says, and the guy in the shades laughs and slips inside. Once he disappears, Dee pushes my shoulders.

"Oh my GOD! Do you know who you were just talking to?!"

I shake my head.

"That was *Adam* EVEREST! He's the lead singer of the band we're here to see!"

An Excerpt from

SINFUL REWARDS 1
A Billionaires and Bikers Novella
by Cynthia Sax

Belinda "Bee" Carter is a good girl; at least, that's
what she tells herself. And a good girl deserves
a nice guy—just like the gorgeous and moody
billionaire Nicolas Rainer. Or so she thinks,
until she takes a look through her telescope
and sees a naked, tattooed man on the balcony
across the courtyard. He has been watching
her, and that makes him all the more enticing.
But when a mysterious and anonymous text
message dares her to do something bad, she
must decide if she is really the good girl she has
always claimed to be, or if she's willing to risk
everything for her secret fantasy of being watched.

An Avon Red Impulse Novella

I'd told Cyndi I'd never use it, that it was an instrument purchased by perverts to spy on their neighbors. She'd laughed and called me a prude, not knowing that I was one of those perverts, that I secretly yearned to watch and be watched, to care and be cared for.

If I'm cautious, and I'm always cautious, she'll never realize I used her telescope this morning. I swing the tube toward the bench and adjust the knob, bringing the mysterious object into focus.

It's a phone. Nicolas's phone. I bounce on the balls of my feet. This is a sign, another declaration from fate that we belong together. I'll return Nicolas's much-needed device to him. As a thank you, he'll invite me to dinner. We'll talk. He'll realize how perfect I am for him, fall in love with me, marry me.

Cyndi will find a fiancé also—everyone loves her—and we'll have a double wedding, as sisters of the heart often do. It'll be the first wedding my family has had in generations.

Everyone will watch us as we walk down the aisle. I'll wear a strapless white Vera Wang mermaid gown with organza and lace details, crystal and pearl embroidery accents, the bodice fitted, and the skirt hemmed for my shorter height. My hair will be swept up. My shoes—

Voices murmur outside the condo's door, the sound piercing my delightful daydream. I swing the telescope upward, not wanting to be caught using it. The snippets of conversation drift away.

I don't relax. If the telescope isn't positioned in the same way as it was last night, Cyndi will realize I've been using it. She'll tease me about being a fellow pervert, sharing the story, embellished for dramatic effect, with her stern, serious dad—or, worse, with Angel, that snobby friend of hers.

I'll die. It'll be worse than being the butt of jokes in high school because that ridicule was about my clothes and this will center on the part of my soul I've always kept hidden. It'll also be the truth, and I won't be able to deny it. I am a pervert.

I have to return the telescope to its original position. This is the only acceptable solution. I tap the metal tube.

Last night, my man-crazy roommate was giggling over the new guy in three-eleven north. The previous occupant was a gray-haired, bowtie-wearing tax auditor, his luxurious accommodations supplied by Nicolas. The most exciting thing he ever did was drink his tea on the balcony.

According to Cyndi, the new occupant is a delicious piece of man candy—tattooed, buff, and head-to-toe lickable. He was completing armcurls outside, and she enthusiastically counted his reps, oohing and aahing over his bulging biceps, calling to me to take a look.

I resisted that temptation, focusing on making macaroni and cheese for the two of us, the recipe snagged from the diner my mom works in. After we scarfed down dinner, Cyndi licking her plate clean, she left for the club and hasn't returned.

Three-eleven north is the mirror condo to ours. I

straighten the telescope. That position looks about right, but then, the imitation UGGs I bought in my second year of college looked about right also. The first time I wore the boots in the rain, the sheepskin fell apart, leaving me barefoot in Economics 201.

Unwilling to risk Cyndi's friendship on "about right," I gaze through the eyepiece. The view consists of rippling golden planes, almost like . . .

Tanned skin pulled over defined abs.

I blink. It can't be. I take another look. A perfect pearl of perspiration clings to a puckered scar. The drop elongates more and more, stretching, snapping. It trickles downward, navigating the swells and valleys of a man's honed torso.

No. I straighten. This is wrong. I shouldn't watch our sexy neighbor as he stands on his balcony. If anyone catches me . . .

Parts 1 – 7 available now!

Parts 1 – 7 available now!

An Excerpt from

FORBIDDEN
An Under the Skin Novel
by Charlotte Stein

Killian is on the verge of making his final vows
for the priesthood when he saves Dorothy from a
puritanical and oppressive home. The attraction
between them is swift and undeniable, but every
touch, every glance, every moment of connection
between them is completely forbidden . . .

An Avon Red Impulse Novel

We get out of the car at this swanky-looking place called Marriott, with a big promise next to the door about all-day breakfasts and internet and other stuff I've never had in my whole life, all these nice cars in the parking lot gleaming in the dimming light and a dozen windows lit up like some Christmas card, and then it just happens. My excitement suddenly bursts out of my chest, and before I can haul it back in, it runs right down the length of my arm, all the way to my hand.

Which grabs hold of his, so tight it could never be mistaken for anything else.

Course I want it to be mistaken for anything else, as soon as he looks at me. His eyes snap to my face like I poked him in the ribs with a rattler snake, and just in case I'm in any doubt, he glances down at the thing I'm doing. He sees me touching him as though he's not nearly a priest and I'm not under his care, and instead we're just two people having some kind of happy honeymoon.

In a second we're going inside to have all the sex.

That's what it seems like—like a sex thing.

I can't even explain it away as just being friendly, because somehow it doesn't feel friendly at all. My palm has been laced with electricity, and it just shot ten thousand volts into him. His whole body has gone tense, and so my body goes tense, but the worst part about it is:

For some ungodly reason he doesn't take his hand away.

Maybe he thinks if he does it will look bad, like admitting to a guilty thing that neither of us has done. Or at least that he hasn't done. He didn't ask to have his hand grabbed. His hand is totally innocent in all of this. My hand is the evil one. It keeps right on grasping him even after I tell it to stop. I don't even care if it makes me look worse—*just let go*, I think at it.

But the hand refuses.

It still has him in its evil clutches when we go inside the motel. My fingers are starting to sweat, and the guy behind the counter is noticing, yet I can't seem to do a single thing about it. Could be we have to spend the rest of our lives like this, out of sheer terror at drawing any attention to the thing I have done.

Unless he's just carrying on because he thinks I'm scared of this place. Maybe he thinks I need comfort, in which case all of this might be okay. I am just a girl with her friendly, good-looking priest, getting a motel room in a real honest and platonic way so I can wash my lank hair and secretly watch television about spaceships.

Nothing is going to happen—a fact that I communicate to the counter guy with my eyes. I don't know why I'm doing it, however. He doesn't know Killian is a priest. He has no clue that I'm some beat-up kid who needs help and protection rather than sordid hand-holding. He probably thinks we're married, just like I thought before, and the only thing that makes that idea kind of off is how I look in comparison.

I could pass for a stripe of beige paint next to him. In here his black hair is like someone took a slice out of the night sky. His cheekbones are so big and manly I could bludgeon the counter guy with them, and I'm liable to do it. He keeps staring, even after Killian says "two rooms please." He's still staring as we go down the carpeted hallway, to the point where I have to ask.

"Why was he looking like that?" I whisper as Killian fits a key that is not really a key but a gosh darn credit card into a room door. So of course I'm looking at that when he answers me, and not at his face.

But I wish I had been. I wish I'd seen his expression when he spoke, because when he did he said the single most startling thing I ever heard in my whole life.

"He was looking because you're lovely."

An Excerpt from

HER HIGHLAND FLING
A Novella
by Jennifer McQuiston

When his little Scottish town is in desperate
straits, William MacKenzie decides to resurrect
the Highland Games in an effort to take
advantage of the new tourism boom and invites
a London newspaper to report on the events.
He's prepared to show off for the sake of the
town, but the one thing William never expects
is for this intrepid reporter to be a she . . .

William scowled. Moraig's future was at stake. The town's economy was hardly prospering, and its weathered residents couldn't depend on fishing and gossip to sustain them forever. They needed a new direction, and as the Earl of Kilmartie's heir, he felt obligated to sort out a solution. He'd spent months organizing the upcoming Highland Games. It was a calculated risk that, if properly orchestrated, would ensure the betterment of every life in town. It had seemed a brilliant opportunity to reach those very tourists they were aiming to attract.

But with the sweat now pooling in places best left unmentioned and the minutes ticking slowly by, that brilliance was beginning to tarnish.

William peered down the road that led into town, imagining he could see a cloud of dust implying the arrival of the afternoon coach. The very *late* afternoon coach. But all he saw was the delicate shimmer of heat reflecting the nature of the devilishly hot day.

"Bugger it all," he muttered. "How late can a coach be? There's only one route from Inverness." He plucked at the damp collar of his shirt, wondering where the coachman could be. "Mr. Jeffers knew the importance of being on time today. We need to make a ripping first impression on this reporter."

James's gaze dropped once more to William's bare legs. "Oh, I don't think there's any doubt of it." He leaned against the posthouse wall and crossed his arms. "If I might ask the question . . . why turn it into such a circus? Why these Games instead of, say, a well-placed rumor of a beastie living in Loch Moraig? You've got the entire town in an uproar preparing for it."

William could allow that James was perhaps a bit distracted by his pretty wife and new baby—and understandably so. But given that his brother was raising his bairns here, shouldn't he want to ensure Moraig's future success more than anyone?

James looked up suddenly, shading his eyes with a hand. "Well, best get those knees polished to a shine. There's your coach now. Half hour late, as per usual."

With a near-groan of relief, William stood at attention on the posthouse steps as the mail coach roared up in a choking cloud of dust and hot wind.

A half hour off schedule. Perhaps it wasn't the tragedy he'd feared. They could skip the initial stroll down Main Street he'd planned and head straight to the inn. He could point out some of the pertinent sights later, when he showed the man the competition field that had been prepared on the east side of town.

"And dinna tell the reporter I'm the heir," William warned as an afterthought. "We want him to think of Moraig as a charming and rustic retreat from London." If the town was to have a future, it needed to be seen as a welcome escape from titles and peers and such, and he did not want this turning into a circus where he stood at the center of the ring.

As the coach groaned to a stop, James clapped William on the shoulder with mock sympathy. "Don't worry. With those bare legs, I suspect your reporter will have enough to write about without nosing about the details of your inheritance."

The coachman secured the reins and jumped down from his perch. A smile of amusement broke across Mr. Jeffers's broad features. "Wore the plaid today, did we?"

Bloody hell. Not Jeffers, too.

"You're late." William scowled. "Were there any problems fetching the chap from Inverness?" He was anxious to greet the reporter, get the man properly situated in the Blue Gander, and then go home to change into something less . . . *Scottish.* And God knew he could also use a pint or three, though preferably ones not raised at his expense.

Mr. Jeffers pushed the brim of his hat up an inch and scratched his head. "Well, see, here's the thing. I dinna exactly fetch a chap, as it were."

This time William couldn't suppress the growl that erupted from his throat. "Mr. Jeffers, don't tell me you *left* him there!" It would be a nightmare if he had. The entire thing was carefully orchestrated, down to a reservation for the best room the Blue Gander had to offer. The goal had been to install the reporter safely in Moraig and give him a taste of the town's charms *before* the Games commenced on Saturday.

"Well, I . . . that is . . ." Mr. Jeffers's gaze swung between them, and he finally shrugged. "Well, I suppose you'll see well enough for yourself."

He turned the handle, then swung the coach door open.

A gloved hand clasped Mr. Jeffers's palm, and then a high, elegant boot flashed into sight.

"What in the blazes—" William started to say, only to choke on his surprise as a blonde head dipped into view. A body soon followed, stepping down in a froth of blue skirts. She dropped Jeffers's hand and looked around with bright interest.

"Your chap's a lass," explained a bemused Mr. Jeffers.

"A lass?" echoed William stupidly.

And not only a lass . . . a very pretty lass.

She smiled at them, and it was like the sun cresting over the hills that rimmed Loch Moraig, warming all who were fortunate enough to fall in its path. He was suddenly and inexplicably consumed by the desire to recite poetry to the sound of twittering birds. That alone might have been manageable, but as her eyes met his, he was also consumed by an unfortunate jolt of lustful awareness that left no inch of him unscathed—and there were quite a few inches to cover.

"Miss Penelope Tolbertson," she said, extending her gloved hand as though she were a man. "R-reporter for the *London Times*."

He stared at her hand, unsure of whether to shake it or kiss it. Her manners might be bold, but her voice was like butter, flowing over his body until it didn't know which end was up. His tongue seemed wrapped in cotton, muffling even the merest hope of a proper greeting.

The reporter was female?

And not only female . . . a veritable goddess, with eyes the color of a fair Highland sky?

He raised his eyes to meet hers, giving himself up to the sense of falling.

Or perhaps more aptly put, a sense of flailing.

"W-welcome to Moraig, Miss Tolbertson."